Wall Of Victory

The Princess Maura Tales
Saga of the de Magela Family

Book Five

Abigail Keam

Worker Bee Press

Worker Bee Press
P.O. Box 485
Nicholasville, KY 40340

Acknowledgements

Thanks to my editor, Faith Freewoman

Artwork by Karin Claesson
www.karinclaessonart.com

Book jacket by Peter Keam
Author's photograph by Peter Keam

Also by Abigail Keam

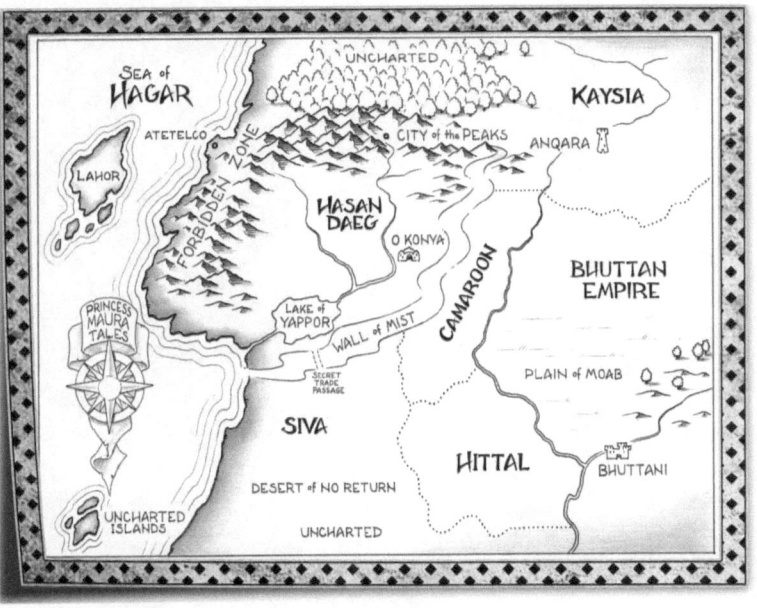

The Princess Maura Series Glossary

Abisola de Magela (character) – ninth queen of Hasan Daeg and mother of Princess Maura

Aga (character) – term for king of the Bhuttanians

Akela (character) – homeless Bhuttanian waif who serves KiKu and Timon

Alexanee (character) – top Bhuttanian general, illegitimate older brother of Dorak

Anqara (place) – ancient cultural and banking city located in country of Kaysia

Atetelco (place) – former capital of the Dinii located in the Forbidden Zone

Beca (character) – Princess Maura's pony

Benzar (character) – gray male hawk from secret society that protects Maura

Bes Amon Ptah (character) – Moab prince hiding under the name of Timon Ben Ibin Moab

Bhutta (character) – female deity of Bhuttanians, wife of Bhuttu

Bhuttan (place) – country ruled by Zoar and his son, Dorak

Bhuttani (place) – capital of Bhuttan

Bhuttanians (characters) – nomadic people who rose to world domination under the leadership of Zoar

Bhuttu (character) – male deity of Bhuttanians whose worship calls for the sacrifice of one's life

Bilboa (characters) – race of people with red eyes who see in the dark

Bird People (characters) – the Dinii who were Overlords of Kaseri

Black Cacodemon (character) – evil wizard of Bhuttu

Blue and gold – royal colors of the Hasan Daegians

Blue Queen (character) – nickname for Maura

Boaeps – small domesticated hopping animals

Borax (both plural and singular) – bison-like animals with sharp blades down their spines

Camaroon (place) – borders Hasan Daeg, absorbed by Bhuttanian Empire

Cappet (character) – petty thief, controls eastern part of Bhuttani

Caromate plant – provides hypnotic mist when leaves are pressed

Chaun Maaun (character) – prince of the Dinii and son of the Dinii Empress Gitar

City of the Peaks (place) – city on top of highest peak in Hasan Daeg where the Dinii live

Colla – nuts from the colla tree, brewed for teas

de Magela (characters) – name of ruling family in Hasan Daeg

Dini (character) – singular of Dinii

Dinii (characters) – ancient rulers of Kaseri, formerly called Overlords, human-like beings covered with feathers who fly

Divigi (character) – spiritual leader of the Dinii and uncle to Empress Gitar

Dorak (character) – son of Zoar, aga of the Bhuttanians

Duchy of Enos (place) – estate passed down through the family of Iasos, husband of Queen Abisola

Duke Enos (character) – father of Iasos

Dyanna (character) – princess born to Maura and Dorak

Everlynd (character) – duchess of Enos and sister of Prince Consort Iasos

Forbidden Zone (place) – former home of the Dinii, cursed by both the Dinii and Hasan Daegians

Gitar (character) – empress of the Dinii and Hasan Daegians

Gootee – duck-like animal

Great Death – name given to the practice of Hasan Daegian queens willing themselves to die

Great Mother – title of respect for older women or those in power, including queens of Hasan Daeg

Hasan Daeg (place) – peaceful agricultural country ruled by the Dinii and the de Magela family

Hasan Daegian betrothal (custom) – woman asks man permission to court by kissing man's hand; if man wishes to engage, he returns the kiss; woman gives man flowers

Hasan Daegians (characters) – peaceful agricultural people who were former slaves of the Dinii

Hetmaan (character) – Bhuttanian term for Spymaster KiKu

Hittal (place) – country conquered by Zoar, land of KiKu the Hetmaan

House of Magi (place) – ancient residence of scholars in Anqara

Iasos (character) – consort of Queen Abisola and father of Princess Maura

Iegani (character) – uncle to Empress Gitar, spiritual advisor to the Dinii, and founder of secret society that protects Princess Maura

Jezra (character) – first wife to Dorak, mother of his first child

Jon (character) – minister to Governor Petenptope of the northern Hasan Daegian state of Kinton

Kaseri (place) – name of the planet

Kaysia (place) – land in which Anqara was located

KiKu (character) – Zoar's Hetmaan, former prince of Hittal who becomes a double spy

KiKusan (character) – daughter of Kiku and concubine of Zoar

Kimtimee (character) – Queen Abisola's highest-ranking general

Kinton (place) – northern region of Hasan Daeg

Kittum (place) – country to the east of Hasan Daeg which has a treaty with Bhuttan

Knoxel (character) – magician who was mentor to Zedek

Land of the Setting Sun (place) – romantic name given to Hasan Daeg by the Bhuttanians

Lahor (place) – former island home of the Lahorians

Lahorians (characters) – originally from Lahor and ancient enemies of the Dinii

Madric (character) – KiKu's first wife

Mamora (character) – first wife of Zoar and sister of KiKu

Maura (character) – tenth ruler of Hasan Daeg, daughter of Queen Abisola and Consort Iasos

Meagan of Skujpor (character) – healer to the royal house of de Magela and member of the House of Magi

Mehmet (character) – high priestess of the House of Magi

Mekonia (character) – nature goddess of the Hasan Daegians

MeNe (character) – Yesemek's first lieutenant

Mikkotto (character) – Hasan Daegian baroness who becomes a traitor and joins with Zoar

Mingo tree – tree with large, flat limbs that is treasured for its endurance, beauty, and strength

Mother Bogazkoy/Royal Bogazkoy – intelligent, self-aware plants that have a special relationship with Hasan Daegian rulers

Nani (character) – adopted granddaughter of Lady Sari

Noabini (character) – Mehmet's assistant who becomes high priestess of the House of Magi

O Konya (place) – capital of Hasan Daeg

Onxor (character) – priest of Bhuttu

Pearl (character) – second wife of KiKu and a healer

Petenptope (character) – governor of the northern Hasan Daegian province of Kinton

Plain of Moab (place) – traditional home of nomadic people

Prosperot (character) – one of two top Bhuttanian generals, along with Alexanee

Qatou (place) – Hasan Daegian city

Rakel (character) – Lahorian woman who helps Princess Maura

Red – royal color of the Bhuttanians

Renna (character) – daughter of Riza

Riza (character) – scion from oldest noble family in Hasan Daeg

Rooshars – rare marsh flower

Rosalind (character) – first queen of Hasan Daeg

Royal Bogazkoy – plant offspring of the Mother Bogazkoy

Rubank (character) – consul to Queen Abisola and then to Queen Maura

Sari (character) – Hasan Daegian nurse to Queen Maura/Queen Abisola and grandmother of Mikkotto and Nani

Shaybar – Bhuttanian drink of boiled water or milk mixed with an equal portion of borax blood

Siddig (character) – Bhuttanian healer who helped Timon

Sinjo – rare berry made into wine that stimulates feelings of pleasure

Siva (place) – desert country south of Hasan Daeg

Sivans (characters) – merchant desert people

Sumsumitoyo (character) – family name of Mikkotto and Sari

Tarsus (character) – gray male hawk Dini who belongs to secret society that protects Maura

Tippa/Tippu (characters) – third and fourth twin wives of KiKu, artists

Tnpothar (character) – Zoar's father

Toppo (character) – red female hawk Dini, belongs to the secret society that protects Maura

Tsnsuni – ritualistic national prayer for the Hasan Daegian queen

Uultepes – mythical animals that are the symbol of Hasan Daegian royalty

Water Orbs – Lahorian mechanical devices constructed for transportation

Wise Ones (character) – title for the Lahorians

Yagomba tree – largest hardwood tree on Kaseri, has mystical powers

Yappor (place) – sacred lake of the Hasan Daegians and thought to be home of their goddess, Mekonia; home to the Lahorians

Yesemek (character) – commander-in-chief of the Dinii and wife to Iegani

Yeti (character) – red female hawk Dini, belongs to secret society that protects Maura

Yubuto (character) – sacrificed son of Mikkotto

Zedek (character) – Black Cacodemon's given name

Zoar (character) – aga (king) of the Bhuttanians

Wall Of Victory

Preface

Maura gathers the reins of power upon the disappearance of the legitimate aga, her husband Dorak. She begins the long trek to Bhuttan to take the capital city and defeat Dorak's first wife, Jezra, who wants the throne for her son, Dorak's firstborn child.

She sends Timon, a scribe, and Prince KiKu, the spylord, to scout the area and report any sightings of Dorak or the Dinii. She believes they may still be alive.

Now at the gates of Bhuttani, Maura is determined to conquer the last remaining rebel holdout.

War has finally come!

1

War!

War came to Bhuttani.

The city, which had wreaked brutal destruction upon Kaseri, was now facing its own ruin.

The great warrior Maura de Magela was coming to claim the throne of the aga with a coalition of battle-hardened Bhuttanians, Hasan Daegians, Anqarians, Camaroons, and mercenaries from within the Empire.

At first, Bhuttanians refused to believe their kinsmen would take up arms against them, but as terrified refugees fled the countryside and flooded the great city with stories of mighty machines which caused the earth to tremble, soldiers as numerous as the stars in the heavens, and a queen with blue skin and unforgiving eyes who pressed relentlessly toward the capital of Bhutan, citizens began to wonder.

"The Blue Queen wants revenge for the death of her parents," they lamented.

Others speculated that she wanted to place her daughter by Dorak in the Bhuttanian Royal Palace.

Still, many carried on as though nothing would interfere their comfortable lives, believing a Bhuttanian soldier would never fight against his own people. "How can a mere girl harden the hearts of Zoar's men against their kinsmen?"

The refugees babbled, "That she-devil sits upon Zoar's throne of bones atop a great platform dragged across the plains by many beasts. Sitting with her are two great felines which act as bodyguards. She is stronger than any giant and swifter than any bird."

"Nonsense," laughed people in the marketplace as they listened to the wild tales of the frightened newcomers.

"You'll see. You'll see," warned the refugees as they begged for food. "The Hasan Daegian women are tall like our men and as strong too. They have no mercy, obeying their queen without question. Even the noble General Alexanee is at her beck and call. The White Queen is no match for the Blue Queen. We'll all be dead before the seasons change."

Many threw coins at the refugees, shaking their heads in disbelief, but as more exiles flooded the city with similar tales, the people became restless and took to the ramparts to study the horizon.

Could it be true? Could a vast army be coming to exact vengeance? Could the Blue Queen raze Bhuttani as they had leveled Anqara?

They didn't have long to ponder.

One night the lookouts spied pinpoints of distant light. Many said it was the fires of the Blue Queen's camp getting closer and closer. Others remarked it was merely the reflection of a moon upon rocks, but all Bhuttanians went to bed troubled and restless.

The next morning their worries intensified when a cloud of dust and smoke spanning many miles arose along the searing horizon across the plain.

A Sivan caravan entered the city with alarmed traders claiming a vast army was burning every house, every barn, every village across a ten-mile swath, while commandeering everything of value and killing anyone who resisted. "The Great Mother is determined to bring Bhuttan to its knees and the capital Bhuttani along with it. Get out while you can," the Sivans advised the terrified citizens.

While many gathered around for news, no one noticed two "Sivans" leaving the caravan and throwing off their desert robes in an alley.

Now dressed as Bhuttanians in ballooning pants and

dark tunics, Pearl and Akela raced toward the temple.

Bedlam had descended into the heart of the city, with merchants closing shops, soldiers marching toward the western gate, and people hoisting children and possessions on their backs, hurrying to escape. Pearl wrestled through the crowd, holding Akela's hand. The escaping throng of citizens grew so unruly, she finally had to pick up the small boy and run with him in her arms. Reaching the portico of an abandoned house, Pearl stopped to rest. She heard looters already at work inside. Putting Akela down, she looked carefully behind her. The last thing she needed was a thug hitting her on the back of the head and stealing Akela for the slave trade.

Pearl squatted down to Akela's level. "Akela, we are only two streets from the temple. You must go and give Empress Maura's message to KiKu. Do you think you can sneak back in?"

Akela glanced at the multitude of people scurrying along the street. He nodded at Pearl with resolve. "I can, Mistress. I know I can."

"Good boy. Repeat the message."

Akela parroted the message that had been drummed into him during the journey back to Bhuttani.

Pearl nodded with relief. "Yes. That's it. Now you must give the message to KiKu and then make your way to the east gate, where the Sivan caravan will be waiting. Can you do that for me?"

Akela nodded, his eyes wide.

"I must go to the inn and collect Madric and Tippu. We will meet at the Sivan caravan. You must be there before the sun vanishes tomorrow or the caravan will leave without you. Do you understand, Akela?"

"I will give the message to KiKu and meet you at the east gate before the sun sets."

"Yes, tomorrow. Do you understand what will happen if you fail to meet us?"

Akela remained silent, thinking of the possibilities.

Pearl grabbed his shoulders. "You will be stuck in this city during the attack. Many people will die if they don't get out. You must be by the east gate by dark tomorrow. Promise me you will be there."

Akela looked into Pearl's worried face and saw the mother he never had, but desired. "I will be there, Mistress. I promise."

Pearl gave a wisp of a smile and kissed the top of Akela's head. "Blessings upon you, child. Be off with you now, and be safe."

Akela judged a space in the crowds where he could push his way through. Within seconds, he was swallowed up by the sea of people scrambling for their lives.

Pearl hoped she would live to see Akela again. Taking a deep breath, she pressed her way into the mob, hoping to find Madric and Tippu safe at the inn. She had to get them out of this city.

Hopefully, KiKu and Timon would be successful in their endeavor. If not, she wondered if the Great Mother would be merciful to KiKu's wives.

One could always wish.

2

Akela pressed through.

He made his way through the city, ducking between legs and squeezing through the crowds until he came to the temple. Hiding behind a refuse bin, he waited until dark. By this time soldiers had established order, and the streets were mostly deserted. Akela stole out from the shadows and scampered into the temple using the route he had taken to escape. Pausing only long enough to allow his eyes adjust to the dim light, he crept along the dark and moldy walls, desperate to make his way to KiKu and deliver the message.

Finding the small oil lamp he had stashed on his way out, Akela fished for the flint he had hidden behind some loose bricks. It took him several minutes to get the damp wick to ignite from striking the flint, but he finally managed. Though the flame from the oil lamp was dim, it illuminated enough to allow Akela to hurry along the damp passageways to KiKu's sleeping room near the wine cellar. KiKu had convinced the priests he could kill more rats if he slept where they kept their nests. They agreed and allowed KiKu to move his pallet into the cellar.

Akela found KiKu resting on his mat near the wine vats. "Master! Wake up!" Akela said while pulling back the ragged blanket, only to find rushes bundled together to resemble a sleeping person.

A hand reached out of the shadows and covered Akela's mouth. "Hush! Do you want to wake the entire complex?"

Akela pulled away from the hand. "Everyone is asleep," he protested, turning to look at KiKu.

"You can never tell who might be listening." KiKu shoved the boy onto his pallet and bit his lip in exasperation. "Akela, tell me the news before I rip out your liver."

Akela gulped. "We met the blue lady with the fancy title. Pearl was afraid of her, I could tell. That made me afraid as well. I didn't like her. Not Pearl, I mean. The blue lady. She didn't have kind eyes."

"Yes, yes, yes," KiKu sighed impatiently. "What did the blue lady say?"

"She kept Tippa, and that made Pearl sad."

"Just tell me what the blue lady *said*, you damned impertinent child!"

Akela sucked in his breath. "Pearl says the empress will strike at the first quarter of the second moon, and you are to get the birds out at all costs. Destroy the temple if you have to, but get them out."

KiKu paced back and forth in his cramped chamber. Stopping suddenly, KiKu grabbed the little boy. "What took you and Pearl so long to get back? Don't you realize our time has all but run out?"

Akela tried to turn his head to escape KiKu's fierce gaze, but KiKu held him so tightly he couldn't. "The caravan had a hard time getting through because of all the people on the roads. There was much thievery and mayhem. With my own eyes, I saw bandits kill an old woman over a bowl of soup. We had to take the long route around."

KiKu exhaled deeply, nodded, and loosened his hold on the boy. "I understand, Akela. I didn't mean to criticize. It's that time is of the essence, but you wouldn't understand, would you? How can a mere boy realize what is at stake?"

"I understand I might get killed."

KiKu chose to ignore Akela's last statement. "Did the blue lady say how we are to use the amulet?"

Akela recited Pearl's message. "As I am blue, press

the stone of the same hue and 'will it.'"

"Will it?"

Akela's eyes grew large at KiKu's menacing expression. "Honest. That's all Mistress Pearl told me to say."

KiKu didn't like the way the boy's eyes darted away from him. "You wouldn't be holding back information for some gold coins?"

"I swear on my mother's grave, that is the message." Akela turned away, but KiKu gripped his arm.

"You little liar. Your mother is probably not dead, and Bhuttanians don't have graves."

"Well, if Bhuttanians don't have graves, what is General Prosperot guarding, then?" asked Akela, drawing himself up.

"Shrines, you fool. Don't you know the difference between a grave and a shrine?"

The boy shook his head. He did not understand why KiKu should be so mean to him when he had risked his life to help. Akela believed he had been very brave, so why was KiKu treating him harshly?

This was the way of the Hittals. They were opportunists with little innate sense of loyalty. Yes, Akela recognized who was standing before him. A man so important that the White Queen would pay handsomely to find him. He could turn KiKu in for a neat profit and buy food for many months.

KiKu's grabbed Akela's throat. "Don't even think it, boy."

"I don't know what you mean," Akela wheezed, grasping at KiKu's iron fingers.

"If I go down, so do the women."

Akela pulled away, rubbing his throat. "I still don't know what you're talking about." Akela was astonished that he could have such a thought. He had come to give the message and then escape with KiKu's wives, who were waiting for him even now. KiKu was right. To betray KiKu was to betray the women, and this Akela would never do. He wanted nothing more than to leave this horrid city before it was overrun with grief and bloodshed. "I would never betray you!"

KiKu grimaced. "One rat recognizes another." He released his grip and tousled the boy's hair. "Stay out of trouble, my young friend. We might make something out of you yet."

Gulping, Akela wondered how long it would be before he could sneak out of the temple and rejoin Pearl.

It couldn't be soon enough for him.

3

Timon was incredulous.

"That's all she had to say? Press the blue stone and 'will it?' Why didn't she tell us this before? We had the amulet and could already have summoned them."

"Perhaps Maura didn't trust us with the information and waited until she had proof the Dinii were in the temple."

Timon curled his hands into fists. "She thought we would betray her to Jezra."

"It was safer if we did not know how to make use of the amulet."

"Who else knows?"

"Until now, only she and the Black Cacodemon knew how to summon the powers of the amulet. The various stones on the amulet command different abilities."

"Such as?"

"I wouldn't know. She didn't entrust that information to me."

"Liar!"

KiKu shrugged. Knowing Timon's nerves were raw, he took no offense at the insult. "The Great Mother and her army will be here within hours, and she wants the Dinii freed. I don't think she's prepared for a long siege. She wants to capture the city quickly."

"Well, why doesn't she ask for one of the moons while she's at it!" Timon uncurled his fists and threw up his hands in disgust.

"She must have identified the feather we sent. We know the Dinii are here. We need to release them. The lives of my wives depend upon it."

"Threats. Threats. Always threats. Why don't we leave? Disappear with the fleeing crowd?"

KiKu drew back. "Too many depend upon us. Besides, Maura would search the world to find us. No, we must do this. We must go to the great hall. That's where the Black Cacodemon was sighted, and where you found the feather."

"What if we release him as well as the Dinii?"

"We must try to kill him. He must not be allowed to come to Jezra's aid."

Resigned to his fate, Timon sighed. "Let's go to

work then. I want to get out of here as soon as possible. This place gives me the chills." He extended his hand. "Give it here."

KiKu blinked at Timon's hand. "Give what here?"

"The amulet, of course."

"I don't have the amulet. I gave it to you."

Timon's eyes widened. "What do you mean? I don't have it. When I awoke, it was gone. I thought you took it for safekeeping."

Timon searched beneath the frayed blanket and tore open the crude straw pallet on KiKu's bed.

KiKu strode around the room at a frantic pace. "Amulets don't get up and walk away!"

"No, they don't, loyal Bilboa, but they can be summoned."

KiKu and Timon looked up to see Hilkiah standing in the doorway. Their eyes caught a multi-colored glimmer below Hilkiah's collarbone.

Timon let out a loud groan.

Hilkiah was wearing the amulet.

A crooked smile spread across the priest's face. "I see thou both dost recognize the sacred amulet. It belongs to Zedek, my mentor and sponsor into the great society of Bhuttu. All magical objects can be summoned. I have felt its presence since ye both joined our community. It has been calling to me in my dreams.

I knew it had to be somewhere in the temple.

"Thou needn't be so aghast, Bilboa. I could have been an apprentice to a cheese guild or a wine merchant or a royal scribe of the Blue Queen, but here I am instead, ready to help my Master."

KiKu murmured to Timon. "That's the extent of Bhuttanian wit for you."

Hilkiah cast a baleful scowl at Timon. "Thou dost not remember me, Prince Bes Amon Ptah, but I remember thee at the court of Zoar. It was just a few occasions when I had to bless something or other at the palace, but thee and thy older brother were present. Just a little thing thou wast, but thee had a peculiar mark on the side of thy neck like this one."

He pointed a finger at a small flower-shaped mole on the back of Timon's neck. "How unfortunate for thee that all novices must shave their hair."

"I don't know what you're talking about, Priest. I am Timon de . . ."

Hilkiah waved his hand. "Save thy breath, young prince. I make no mistake." He slowly inched closer to KiKu. "I am puzzled about thee, though I think thou wast Zoar's man. I never got a good look, as thou wast always lurking in the shadows just out of sight."

KiKu struck his hand out quickly, but Hilkiah jerked his head back. KiKu's hands were met by an angry purple shield, stinging him terribly. He jumped, cradling his singed hand. "Damn you, Priest!"

Hilkiah turned to Timon. "Well, it is clear this man is no Bilboa. It doth not matter. We shall soon have the truth out of thee."

"What do you mean?" Timon asked.

"He means you are going to tell us everything hidden inside your insipid skull," said Mikkotto, stepping into the small sleeping cell.

Timon's eyes narrowed. "Who are you?"

Mikkotto lounged against the doorjamb, slapping her gloves against her thigh. She righted herself and strode over, pressing her lean body against him.

"Stay away. Don't touch me," squeaked Timon.

"Settle down," purred Mikkotto as she stroked the boy's cheek. She leaned into Timon's face until her lips glanced off his. "Very comely in the face. I did not expect you to be so appealing, but you are a tad thin for my taste." Mikkotto's eyes unhurriedly traveled down Timon's body as her hands wandered below his waist.

Timon recoiled from her touch.

Chuckling, Mikkotto reached out and grabbed Timon's tunic, pulling him to her. "I am Baroness Mikkotto from the House of Sumsumitoyo—a royal cousin of the House of de Magela. Surely you have heard of me?"

Timon felt deep fear. "I've heard of you."

"Yes, I can see in your eyes that you have."

"Baroness, we must not keep Aganess Jezra waiting," Hilkiah said nervously.

Ignoring the priest, Mikkotto pulled Timon even closer. "How fares Lady Maura?"

"You mean the pretender? I do not know, Baroness."

Mikkotto smiled. "Come, come now. Make it easy on yourself, Prince Bes. You can tell us what we want to know and dine sumptuously tonight, or you can suffer unspeakable pain and still tell us what we want to know. The choice is yours."

"I don't know what you want of me."

"We have the amulet. We know you work for Maura. We just want to know why."

"Why what?"

Mikkotto asked, "Why did she entrust the amulet to you and permit you to bring it into the temple of Bhuttu? Why would Maura run the risk of the amulet being discovered? Surely she must have realized the priests would sense the presence of the amulet. It doesn't make sense, my young man."

Hilkiah stepped forward. "We needed the amulet to set Zedek free, so why would she allow the amulet to leave her control?"

"You know where Zedek is?" gasped KiKu in a sarcastic tone.

"Silence! No one gave thee permission to speak," hissed Hilkiah. "Lashes across thy back will cure thee of thy insolence."

Mikkotto smiled. "I don't think I would waste my time on the Bilboa. My guess is no torture would be effective on him."

"Why not?" sneered Hilkiah.

"Because while you have been babbling, he has swallowed something. Probably poison."

Timon jerked free from Mikkotto and raced to KiKu. "Don't let it be true!" He peered into KiKu's strained face. "Don't leave me alone with these villains!"

KiKu's eyes rolled up into his head.

Grabbing KiKu's tunic, Timon began shaking him, "You coward! How could you?"

"I . . . was . . . commanded to . . ." gasped KiKu, slipping into unconsciousness and slowly sliding to the floor.

Timon caught the collapsing spylord and held him, weeping against the KiKu's neck. "Don't leave me! You can't abandon me!"

KiKu shook violently several times and went limp. His still-open eyes stared back at Timon as his mouth went slack and a thin trail of blood oozed from his mouth and down his chin.

Timon let out a piercing cry that filled the small chamber and echoed down the long hallway, holding KiKu tightly to his breast.

Mikkotto closed her eyes for a brief instant while she savored KiKu's death. She learned long ago that death was a useful tool in achieving her goals and vanquishing her enemies, even if it meant using her children as assassins—well, her male children.

Her daughters must survive at all costs. She had left them in hiding with a trusted relative in Hasan Daeg, where they awaited her triumphant return.

She straightened her pose while inserting her gloves into her belt, then beckoned to a sentry standing outside the cell. "When the boy stops weeping, bring him to the aganess. She wants to question him."

The guard returned the Bhuttanian salute and stood in the doorway.

Hilkiah squeezed past the large sentry to follow Mikkotto as she swaggered out of the cellar.

"What shall we do now?" asked the High Priest.

Mikado turned a lazy gaze upon the anxious, pale man. "If I were you, I would be making up a good story."

"What dost thou mean?"

"The boy's servant killed himself with poison. If he

truly was Zoar's traitorous hetmaan, the aganess will not be pleased to learn of his death. He would have been a fountain of information."

Hilkiah's face became livid with red streaks rushing up his neck onto his cheeks. His eyebrows arched high while his mouth took on an unpleasant shape. "Thou wast present as well. I wasn't the only one standing by while that creature swallowed poison."

Mikkotto smiled. "Not my temple. Not my responsibility." She pointed to the priest's chest. "I don't think the aganess will appreciate that you revealed the amulet." She whispered into his ear. "I believe it was to remain a secret. Now I'll have to kill the sentry in case he overheard."

"Oh, great Bhuttu!" exclaimed Hilkiah, grabbing Mikkotto's arm.

She scowled disdainfully at his chalky hand.

Hilkiah removed his hand quickly and pleaded, "Canst thou not help me? Of course, I would assist any endeavor thou seest fit in the near future, perhaps?" Hilkiah's voice had taken on a silky quality.

Mikkotto smiled. "I can think of something you can do for me right now. Let us return to your chambers and discuss it."

Hilkiah's smirk faded, since he knew of Mikkotto's reputation for deriving pleasure from engaging in practices that could prove painful to others, but he did not wish to anger the powerful woman. "It would be my honor, Baroness," Hilkiah assured, thinking he would just have to endure whatever Mikkotto had in store for him.

"After you," responded Mikkotto, bowing before the priest. As Hilkiah trudged to his chambers, Mikkotto signaled to her entourage waiting in the hallway.

They nodded.

When the two were out of sight, Mikkotto's Hasan Daegian women stormed the room, garroted the sentry, pulled Timon off KiKu's lifeless body, and spirited him away into the misty gloom.

4

"Where is the boy now?"

"Outside, awaiting your command," Mikkotto replied.

"What could I possibly want with him?" sneered Jezra, popping a sweet wafer into her mouth.

Mikkotto's golden brown eyes narrowed. "I don't know. I thought perhaps you would like to interrogate him, since he came here at Maura's behest, and her forces are practically on our doorstep."

Jezra delicately wiped her mouth with a lace napkin. "I know all I need to know," she answered with smug satisfaction.

"Really?"

"I observed what took place in the temple's cellar."

Mikkotto began to slowly circle Jezra. "How is that, my sweet?"

Jezra dropped the napkin to her lap in exasperation. "I hope you don't think your stalking intimidates me, because it doesn't, so sit down." She reached for another wafer, which Mikkotto swept out of her hand.

Jezra glared at the broken wafer on the floor. "Look what you have done, you stupid Hasan Daegian! You people have no manners. None. You're just like these crude Bhuttanians. Barbarians! The lot of you!"

"I want to know the meaning of your comment. Why do you say that you know all you need to know?"

Jezra smiled sweetly and replied in a voice full of venom. "I know what you think of me. I know what all you barbarians think of me, but I will reign as queen. Oh yes, I will. I will rule, and use Bhuttanians as slaves to rebuild Anqara, and she will rise from the ashes to be greater than ever. I swear I will. I swear it," she said, throwing a wafer at Mikkotto.

"And I will help you," offered Mikkotto. She gently stroked Jezra's hair. "But first things first. What do you know, and how did you learn of it? Demonstrate to me just how dim-witted I am in the presence of an imposing Anqarian."

Jezra spread her diaphanous red skirts out and played with their pleats. "I am able to conjure up sights," she said with some satisfaction.

"Is this something Zedek showed you?"

"Yes," replied Jezra, now smoothing the bodice of her dress.

Mikkotto frowned. She wondered if Jezra's childlike behaviors were more worrisome than simple immaturity. She feared the aganess was losing her mind due to the stress of the civil war.

"Show me," Mikkotto coaxed.

"Really?"

"Yes, really. I am always impressed by magic."

Jezra nodding with delight, sat straight up on the divan, mumbled an unintelligible incantation, and waved her hands in a circular motion. The air thickened and blackened, as if with smoke.

Mikkotto reached out to touch the wavering air, but was repulsed by a thick vibration that singed the hair on her arm. Fearing she had been burned, Mikkotto pulled back in alarm and checked her arm.

"Now watch closely when the circle begins to clear," Jezra advised.

Mikkotto watched in amazement. She had never really gotten over the Hasan Daegians' distrust of magic, but she had to admit to herself its use excited her. Peering closely, she saw the black circle clear to a yellowish, shimmering mist.

"Here it comes now," said Jezra. Giggling, she tucked her legs and feet under her on the divan. Slowly the image of Timon and Mikkotto talking began to emerge as though Jezra had been present in KiKu's small chamber. The image swung around to Hilkiah and then to the Bilboa.

"The vision is fading. Can you brighten it?" asked Mikkotto.

"No. I grow tired. I find it difficult when I am fatigued."

"You were observing us the entire time?"

"Yes." Jezra thought for a moment. "I am surprised, Baroness. I hesitated to share my talent with you because I thought you would be angry."

"Angry? Quite the contrary. I think it is wonderful. With this gift, you can spy into Maura's tent. We can overhear her consulting with her generals and learn of their plans for attacking the city."

Jezra shook her head slowly. "My power has only a very limited distance. I am unable to go beyond the city walls, much less venture into Maura's encampment."

Mikkotto's face fell. "Why can't anything be easy?" she said to no one in particular.

"I am sorry," said Jezra earnestly. "I only studied with Zedek for a short time." Tears welled in her eyes.

Mikkotto eased down onto a stool. "Why did you study with that odious creature, anyway?"

Jezra wiped her tears with her lace napkin. "I wanted

the power to bring harm to Dorak."

"Oh, is that all?"

Jezra looked surprised. "It is everything, Mikkotto. I can see you have never been in love. You don't understand how the loss of love can bring utter devastation. It can twist someone's mind. I hardly recognize myself sometimes. I used to be so full of gaiety and happiness. Now I am the lowest of the low." She stared at her hands folded in her lap.

"Why don't you just put Dorak out of your mind and forget him?"

"That's what most people would say, but that is the curse of love. One can't forget. You become consumed with the loss. I've tried. I can't move on, so I want only to hurt him the way he has wounded me."

"Dorak is dead, Jezra. He is gone, and beyond your ability to bring harm to him."

The pale-haired girl shook her head. "I don't feel it. I sense his presence, his life force. He is alive somewhere. I know it."

Mikkotto said nothing, thinking it best not to respond. The pain of others was usually nothing to her, but she felt sad for this young girl who had been so badly used by powerful men.

"Have you never been in love, Mikkotto?"

Mikkotto's mouth turned down, and she wearily

rubbed her forehead. "When I was very young, I was in love."

"What happened to him?"

"He died," replied Mikkotto, slowly recalling that long-ago time in her life.

"What happened to your beloved?"

"He committed suicide."

"Oh!"

Mikkotto rose to her feet. "He died by his own hand after my mother arranged my marriage to another man. My husband's family was very wealthy, and my mother wanted his estate. To exact my revenge, I made my husband's life so miserable, he committed suicide, too."

"Was it really suicide?"

"It was ruled as such."

"I see."

"I suppose you do."

"Truly, I am sorry," Jezra said.

Mikkotto shrugged. "I am going to check on our young friend waiting in the hallway." She strode to the door and stopped. Without looking back at Jezra, she said softly, "You are right. Loss of love does change a person, and not for the better, I'm afraid."

She was going to prove it now. The baroness was determined to get the truth out of the young Prince of Moab, even if she had to slowly flay him inch by inch.

With the knowledge she gleaned, she would capture the daughter of Queen Abisola de Magela, her cousin and kinswoman, take the usurper's place, and become queen of Hasan Daeg. She then would have Jezra poisoned and establish a subservient puppet to rule Bhuttan.

Secure in her power, Mikkotto ordered for Timon to be taken to the deepest subterranean reaches of the Imperial Palace. She did not want to be disturbed while the young prince was "coaxed" to give up his secrets.

Isolated in the catacombs, Mikkotto never received early reports that Maura was now a mere stone's throw from the city.

She was too busy . . . with Timon.

5

Akela awoke.

Lying on a pile of cloth bags stored in the cellar where the root vegetables were kept, he listened. A half-eaten tuber fell out of his clutched fingers. Sitting up, he shook away the cobwebs of sleep. Where was he? Then he remembered. He had been hungry, so instead of going to his assigned pallet in one of the outer rooms near the kitchen, Akela had stolen into the root cellar and stuffed his tummy with tubers until he fell asleep. Now Akela was awake and listening to a myriad of footfalls running about the temple.

Something had happened!

Had the blue lady entered the city?

Akela strained to listen. There were no screams—just people moving about upstairs quickly and dragging things across the floor. He decided people were moving furniture and boxes.

Why?

Were they looking for him?

Akela jumped up from his pallet of rags and lit his small lamp. Feeling his way along the wall, he found the entrance to the secret passageways and hurried down one of them to uncover the novice's robe and sandals he had stashed in one of the anterooms.

If the temple authorities were searching for him, the disguise should make it hard for them to find him. As soon as Akela slipped into the novice's robe, he would look like hundreds of other little boys serving in the temple complex. And he could always escape into the secret passageways, which he knew like the back of his hand. He had spent many hours exploring them with KiKu.

KiKu!

Perhaps Akela should find KiKu or Timon and ask them what was happening and see if it was time for him to join Pearl and the other wives.

Yes, that is what he would do!

6

Mikkotto wiped away her sweat.

"Tell me what you know, and your pain will stop. Otherwise, this will go on until I get what I want."

Stripped of his clothes, Timon struggled against the chains binding his wrists. He hung from the ceiling, his toes barely touching the floor. He never dreamed a person could be in such agony and still be conscious, much less alive. "I tell you again. I don't know anything. I'm a nobody."

"You are Prince Bess Amon Ptah—a royal. Your people would never have allowed you to abdicate to become a mere priest of Bhuttu, but you might have been sent on a mission by the pretender. Now, I ask you again. Why were you sent here?"

Timon tried to laugh, but his voice could only manage a sound resembling a raspy horn. "I . . . don't . . .

know who this Ptah is. My name is Timon Ben Ibin of Moab. I am the son of a wealthy barley farmer."

Mikkotto snorted, "Oh, stop this nonsense. There are no barley farms in Moab. You've changed the story of who you are so many times that even you are confused." Mikkotto plunged an iron rod into a blazing fire. "Maybe a white-hot poker can release the truth from your tongue. You think about that while it warms up."

Timon stared at the metal rod as it began to glow red, then orange, and finally a white-blue flame. In the waves of intense heat, the poker seemed to dance from side to side. He realized he couldn't keep up the pretense much longer. He was going to crack. He knew it, and what was worse still, Timon realized Mikkotto knew it too.

He could only hope he had given Maura enough time to move her soldiers into place around the city walls. Although he had failed to find the Dinii, Timon hoped Maura would have mercy on his people and KiKu's wives. His parched voice could only manage a faint whisper, "Have mercy, Great Mother."

"What was that?" asked Mikkotto, looking up from stirring the poker in the searing embers. "What did you say?"

Timon's head drooped, and his chin rested on his

chest. His body twitched uncontrollably. Mikkotto dropped the poker and grabbed Timon's legs, taking the pressure off his swollen wrists. She turned to the sentries standing guard behind her. "Help me, you fools. Can't you see he's trying to swallow his tongue!" she cried to the guards.

The guards rushed over and undid the chains binding Timon's wrists. They let him down with a loud thump while one of them pried open Timon's mouth and pulled on his tongue while another one roughly inserted a round piece of wood between his teeth. Mikkotto stood over Timon in a blind rage. "Get him breathing again. He is not to die until I've finished with him."

She nervously paced the floor around Timon's limp form until a healer rushed into the room. She watched intently as the healer administered a stimulant.

Seconds later, Timon's eyes fluttered open, and he begged for water.

The guards looked at Mikkotto, questioning.

She nodded.

A guard wet a rag from his personal flask of water and squeezed it over Timon's mouth.

Timon coughed at first, but then greedily gulped the water.

"This boy is too weak. Any more torture and he will

die," the healer cautioned Mikkotto, barely concealing his distaste. He lowered his eyes, fearing Mikkotto could sense his loathing. He knew of her reputation and did not want to become her next victim.

Mikkotto shot the healer a look of extreme irritation, but did not tarry long with him because a courier rushed into the dungeon. Giving Mikkotto a salute and falling to one of his knees, he bowed his head and extended his arm to hand her a sealed report.

"I said I was not to be disturbed," hissed Mikkotto, striking the courier.

The courier kowtowed. "I beg your forgiveness, Mistress, but I was charged with delivering this bulletin to you upon pain of death should I fail." He pulled a dagger from his belt and offered the hilt to Mikkotto.

Mikkotto swept the dagger to the floor in irritation, knowing that if her orders had been disobeyed the report had to be of vast importance. Her heart thumped wildly.

Grabbing the report, Mikkotto hurried over to a sconce to examine it in the flickering light. Recognizing the official wax insignia, she quickly broke the seal. "You, there," she called to the healer. "Come here and read this to me."

The surprised healer gingerly took the report from Mikkotto and scanned it quickly.

"It must be bad news from the expression on your face. Mind you, be careful and whisper so only I will hear what is written."

The healer leaned over and, cupping Mikkotto's ear, reported the details of the report in a faint, trembling voice.

If Mikkotto was alarmed, her expression did not betray it. She snatched the report from the man's shaky hand and thrust it into the burning embers that still held the poker. "Stay with your patient, healer. If he dies, you will share his fate."

The healer bowed so low he nearly toppled over. "I'll do my best, Great Lady."

"Pray, my good man, your best will be good enough. I make no idle threats."

A guard standing behind Mikkotto chuckled faintly.

Mikkotto swirled around in a flash of anger. "You guards, go immediately to the west gate." She looked at the courier. "Go with them."

The courier, relieved that he was not going to die at the hands of this foreign woman, jumped up and ran out of the dungeon.

"We are waiting upon your pleasure, Great Lady. We don't want to lock you in," said the senior officer.

Grabbing her gloves from her belt, Mikkotto stormed up the stone staircase and out of the dungeon.

The guards grabbed their weapons. "What was in the message, old man?" one of them asked.

The healer cautioned, "You'd better hurry. How do you know she's not listening from the hall?"

"Let's go," barked the officer. "The old man may be right. Whatever it was, it couldn't have been good."

A subordinate complained, "It doesn't matter one way or another. We're all going to meet our deaths."

"That's what we do. We're soldiers. I'd rather die in battle standing on my feet than be an old man pissing in my pants," his superior replied.

The officer waited until all the others had stomped up the stairs. He slammed the iron door shut and shoved the rusty key into place. Peering down into the chamber through the bars in the door, he made a quick decision.

Watching down the dank corridor until he was confident his brothers-in-arms had rounded the corner, the guard took the key and threw it between the iron bars. It landed on the bare stone floor with a loud clang.

Startled by the sudden noise, the healer looked up, and his eyes fell upon the worn key. Glancing at the door, he saw the guard standing with his arm still between the bars.

Nodding to the old man, the guard gave a ghost of a smile, quickly withdrew his arm, and hurried to join his comrades.

The old man rushed over and grabbed the key, kissing it. Then he snatched up the courier's dagger.

The gods had consented to give him and the young prisoner a reprieve. He wondered who the young man was, to be granted such divine favor. It surely wasn't due to him.

The old man shook his head. It didn't matter. What mattered was getting the youth and himself away from the palace.

The boy looked too heavy for him to carry any great distance. The healer did not want to leave him, but would if he had to. The young man had to get to his feet and be able to move.

He simply had to.

7

Maura sat astride Dorak's black steed.

Beside her was Alexanee, mounted on another massive warhorse. They were on a promontory studying the city.

"Do you think Bhuttani will surrender? I don't want a bloodbath."

Alexanee's horse shifted its weight, which gave him time to evaluate the question. "Great Mother, I hope they do, but knowing the Bhuttanian mindset as I do, I'm sure my brothers will fight to the death."

Maura pondered Alexanee's words. "That is not my wish. They are guided by a weak ruler. Surely Jezra will not challenge me."

"She must resist, Great Mother, for she knows it will mean death for her son and herself if she surrenders. Jezra will fight, for she has no alternative."

"I would consider showing mercy and allowing them to live. We could communicate this to her."

Alexanee scoffed, "Where? What kind of life? An austere existence in some dark prison in a faraway province, where they'd have contact with only their guards?"

"It's better than dying."

"Is it?"

Maura turned in her saddle to face Alexanee. "What troubles you, General? You've never spoken so harshly to me before."

Alexanee glanced momentarily at the city below and then looked back at Maura. "May I be frank, Great Mother?"

"I expect you to be so always."

"The fact that tomorrow I will rain fury down upon the capital of my homeland makes me quiver with such revulsion I can barely stand it."

"Revulsion, yes, but misgivings? Is your loyalty compromised?"

Alexanee looked once more at the city before responding. His forearms flexed as his grip on the horse's reigns tightened. "It must be done, I'm sorry to say."

"Yes, we agree it must be done if the world is to recover. Jezra must not hold the reins of Bhuttanian power any longer. She will bleed the world dry if not deposed."

Alexanee nodded.

"Give the signal, General."

Alexanee closed his eyes for a moment. He knew Maura was watching him. The Blue Queen was right, though. This had to be done, but how he dreaded the thought of killing his people. He raised his hand and gave the signal to set up camp.

Tomorrow, when the two moons had set and dawn broke, the combined forces of Maura's army would conquer Bhuttani, and the world as Alexanee knew it would cease to exist.

Grunting her approval and giving a curt nod, Maura turned her horse around and cantered away.

Alexanee remained behind, staring at Bhuttani and knowing tomorrow the Bhuttanian Empire would be no more.

8

Akela searched everywhere.

He searched Timon's small cell. He searched the alcove where KiKu slept. He searched all the halls where KiKu might be working. He searched the main chambers where the novices prayed. He searched the empty kitchen. Finally he went back to explore the cellar.

It was all the small boy could do to shove panic back down his throat. He wanted to scream with fear, and struggled mightily to appear calm whenever he encountered anyone.

Had the real identities of Timon and KiKu been discovered? Knowing their quest was doomed to fail, and fearing the blue lady, had Timon and KiKu cut and run, deserting him? Were KiKu's wives waiting for him by the east gate, or was that a ruse to get rid of him?

Akela ran from room to room. He searched the entire kitchen and cellar region, all except one room where the cooks stored vinegar and hard cider. Akela tried the door. Locked! That was strange. This room had never been locked before. He would know, since he had fetched buckets of vinegar many a time for KiKu, who used it in hot water to scrub away mold in the dank rooms of the temple.

He shook the doorknob. The door rattled on its rusty hinges, but it would not open. "Master? Are you in there?" whispered the boy.

Silence was his only answer.

Akela studied the door and the lock. The lock was nothing more than more than a flimsy strip of metal which slid into a roughly carved-out niche in the doorjamb. He had heard it referred to as a lover's lock. It should be simple to open.

Determined to get into the room, he looked around for something to pry the door open. In a corner, the boy spotted a small rusty knife that had been used to peel root vegetables, probably left by some careless boy like himself.

Akela smiled. He knew he could open the door with the knife. He hadn't survived on the streets all his life just by begging. Sometimes he had broken into a rich man's house at night, stuffing himself and his pockets with sweetmeats and soft rolls and left before footsteps sounded on the floor above him.

He inserted the knife into the keyhole and deftly turned the blade. Nothing happened. Akela frowned. He tried jimmying the lock again, this time putting more pressure on the knife. The blade broke. Akela took a step back, astonished. Such a thing had never happened to him before. The young boy felt tears burn his eyes and spill down his cheeks. He wiped them away with the hem of his now-dirty yellow robe. Not knowing what else to do, Akela sat upon a sack filled with grain and stared at the knife handle with its broken blade, pondering.

He remembered a gang he used to shadow before the older boys ran him off. He was glad they did, since they were cruel and pinched his share of food, but he remembered how one of the lads inserted a knife between the lock and the doorjamb when they broke into a bakery for some honey cakes.

Akela looked at his broken blade. Maybe there was enough metal that he could use the same technique. He hopped off the sack and went over to the door. This would be his last attempt to find KiKu. If this failed, he would give up his search, sneak out of the temple, and hurry to the east gate where the caravan and safety awaited him.

Gingerly, Akela inserted the broken blade into the niche. He jiggled the knife until the blade caught on something. Hoping it had caught on the lock, Akela pressed the blade to the left, causing it to move right. Slowly he felt the lock give way. He adjusted the knife and pressed some more. The metal of the lock slid back somewhat to the right.

Feeling confident, Akela put more pressure on the knife handle, causing the door to squeak. Grabbing hold of the grimy, wooden handle, he pulled. The door creaked open.

Akela peered inside but saw nothing, as it was pitch black inside. Usually-lit torches in the room were extinguished. Gathering his small lamp, Akela lit a torch by the door.

Blowing the lamp out, he took the torch and placed it in a stand inside the room. Looking about the storage room, Akela's heart sank. There was nothing but wooden barrels of cider and earthenware urns of vinegar stacked floor to ceiling. KiKu was not here, and Akela had no other place to look. He had failed Pearl. Akela's thoughts immediately turned to the city and joining the caravan. There was nothing left to do but save himself. He hoped KiKu's wives would understand and let him stay with them.

Akela's ears perked up, catching a faint sound behind some wooden barrels of cider in a dusty corner. Poised to flee in case he encountered a huge rat, Akela peered over the barrels and discovered a long bundle wrapped in a burial shroud. He shrank from the sight, but then thought better of it.

Why would the Bhuttu priests conceal a dead body in the vinegar cellar with the door locked? Death was a celebration for the adherents of Bhuttu—not something clouded in secrecy and hidden away.

Akela heard a noise again, and it sounded like a weak moan. He inched closer and prodded the bundle with his foot.

The bundle twitched.

Akela poked the heap on the floor again, this time harder. He was greeted with a muffled cry followed by a stream of obscenities.

Akela immediately recognized the voice. "Master!" he cried, taking his rusty, battered knife and carefully cutting away rope from the shroud until KiKu's face emerged.

KiKu sputtered, "Water!"

Akela surveyed the storeroom. "There's no water here."

"Wine, then. Find me something to drink."

Akela frantically sawed the knife back and forth to release KiKu's hands.

"Careful, you little alley boaep. Do you want to slash my wrists? Face the blade away from my hands."

Akela freed KiKu's hands and dropped the knife as he ran to search for something to drink. He hurried to the wine vault and, snatching the sampling cup the kitchen staff used to taste the wine, he rushed back to the vinegar cellar. Yanking the cork from a barrel, he filled the wooden cup with hard cider.

By this time KiKu had managed to free his feet and was on his hands and knees, feebly trying to stand up. "Help me, boy," he muttered.

Akela placed the cider on a small table and rushed to KiKu's side, distressed at seeing the spylord so weak and disoriented. "Put your hands on my shoulders," suggested Akela. "I will help you stand."

Pressing his weight against Akela's small frame, KiKu finally managed to rise. "I'm getting too damned old for this," he grumbled.

Wobbly, but erect at last, KiKu leaned against some shelves. "Just give me a minute while I catch my breath."

Akela handed him the cup filled with cider.

KiKu drank it all in one gulp. "Nice and cool," he said to no one in particular. Turning his attention to Akela, he asked, "Has the city been attacked? Tell me, lad, what is our situation?"

Akela replied, "No, Master, but the blue lady is not far. We see lights from her camp."

KiKu grunted in Bhuttanian fashion. "Good. That means we still have time." He paused in thought. "Master Timon?"

Akela shrugged.

KiKu nodded. "It's up to me." He placed a hand on the boy's shoulder. "You have done well, but it's time for you to leave, Akela. Join my wives and flee the city. Tell them to honor my memory by living full and happy lives. All that was mine is now theirs for the taking."

"Are you not coming? What about Master Timon?"

KiKu assured him, "I will find him, and if fate permits, we will join you outside the city, but you must go now. Find my wives and tell them what I said. You won't forget?"

Akela parroted the message. "Honor you by living happy lives."

KiKu smiled sadly. "Go now, Akela."

Akela looked at the shroud shredded on the floor. "Were you dead, Master?"

"No, my boy. I was playing dead. A trick I learned using a special herb."

"Will you teach me how to play dead, too?"

"Be off with you, Akela." KiKu pushed Akela away.

Akela started for the door, but stopped. "Maybe I

should stay with you. You seem weak."

KiKu threw the wooden cup at him. "LEAVE! I HAVE NO NEED OF YOU!"

Akela shot KiKu a wounded look before rushing out the door. It was all he could do not to cry.

KiKu stared at the empty doorway. "Goodbye, my little thief. May the gods bless you and keep you safe." Resigned to his fate, KiKu picked the rusty knife up off the floor "This will do nicely. Very nicely, indeed!"

9

T imon was too weak to go far.

Getting Timon safely out of the dungeon was a slow and arduous process, leaving the healer exhausted. He gently set Timon down on the stone floor against a wall near the palace stables. "I'm sorry, my friend, but I can do no more. We must get help."

Timon clutched the old man's hand. "I must get to the temple of Bhuttu. It is of the utmost importance."

"You're in no condition to travel on your own. We must find a place where you can hide. Then I will take my leave of you to gather my household and escape the city."

Shaking his head and tightening his grip on the healer's arm, Timon insisted, "I must go to the temple. Many lives depend upon it. Can you give me something? A stimulant? I need to get back on my feet."

The healer shook his head. "I know of no herb or medicine that would help you in your condition."

"You must have something in the pouch that you're wearing. Please. If I don't finish my mission, the Blue Queen will tear this city apart looking for Aga Dorak."

"The aga? He is dead. No one has seen him for a very long time. It is believed one of his wives had him assassinated, probably the very queen you speak of." The healer looked troubled. "What has going to the temple got to do with the aga?"

"We think the Black Cacodemon put a spell on Dorak and he is trapped in the temple of Bhuttu."

The healer spat on the ground contemptuously. "Zoar banned that accursed demon, but rumors abound that Dorak brought the pestilence back into the world."

"It's true. With my own eyes, I saw the wizard materialize at Zoar's funeral. Dorak released him to do his bidding, but the wizard, in turn, hexed Dorak. We think he is in the temple, held there by black magic."

"So the Blue Queen did not kill Dorak?"

"No, and neither did the White Queen."

"Who is 'we?'"

"I am in the service of the Blue Queen."

The healer recoiled and spat again. "Traitor! Why should I help a false claimant who wants to destroy my country?"

"The Blue Queen wants to find Dorak, not kill him."

"Foolish knave. How can you be taken in by her deceit? Everyone knows she seeks to install her daughter on the throne."

"The Blue Queen will unite this city and bring an end to all this bloodshed and suffering. All of Dorak's generals support her, even the powerful Alexanee, and they are willing to fight their kith and kin to bring an end to this senseless civil war. The world is dying. The Blue Queen is our last hope of salvation."

Rubbing his eyes, the healer slumped against the wall. "I am near my time of leaving this world. All is in chaos. This city, my home, is on the brink of annihilation. What to do? What to do?"

Timon squeezed the old man's hand. "Help me to bring an end to this carnage, I beg of you."

The healer finally nodded. "I can give you something that will give you strength, but I warn you—it will affect your heart. Once it wears off, your heart will be irreparably damaged."

"Give it to me! I must have it!"

"The dangers."

Timon tried to straighten, but fell back against the wall. "I must be off. I must find my friend and finish my mission."

"You swear to me upon all that is holy that your queen will set things right?"

"You have no idea how powerful she is. She has the strength of ten men and is swift like a bird in flight, yet there is good in her. Wherever her forces have been, law has been established, trade routes connected, and the land has begun to recover from Zoar's policy of slash and burn. The Blue Queen will do more good than harm. But I tell you this—she is determined to capture the throne, and she will do anything to accomplish this. Believe me when I tell you, Jezra is no match for Maura de Magela."

The healer studied Timon's face for what seemed like a long time, looking for deceit. At last, he decided. "I will help you. My name is Siddig. Remember me in your prayers, and make it known to your queen how I aided you, and implore her to have mercy on my family."

Timon said, "Look inside the pocket of this robe."

The healer prodded the pocket of the dirty robe he had found on the dungeon floor and used to clothe Timon. Rummaging through the frayed pocket, he pulled out a child's wooden signet ring with a borax bull carved on it.

"If the Blue Queen does not honor you, take this ring to the nomads on the steppes. Find the mother of

Prince Bes Amon Ptah and give her this ring. She will honor any request from you. This is my word."

The old man's eyes widened as he recognized the symbol of royalty from the people who lived on the grasslands. He bowed in respect. "My lord."

"Now give me the stimulant. We've no time to lose."

The old man fished inside his pouch and pulled out several dried leaves. "Take only a little as needed. It will take away any pain and give you immense energy, but each leaf you chew will weaken your heart until nothing, not even this sacred plant, can help you."

Timon's hand trembled as he grabbed the leaves from the healer's hands.

"Only a little bit of the leaf at a time. Chew until pulpy, and then swallow quickly. Remember—a little at a time."

Timon had trouble pulling a leaf apart, so the healer tore a section and put it on Timon's tongue. Immediately Timon felt a surge of energy. He sat up. "This is marvelous. I feel rejuvenated."

"Do not be beguiled, my friend. This plant loves to seduce as she steals life from your heart."

Timon grabbed the old man's hand and shook it. "Thank you. You have saved my life and countless others."

The healer nodded and rising, took his leave with grave misgivings, convinced he had doomed the young man to an early death.

But there would be many deaths in the coming days, and many young men and women would die before their time.

Their fate was written in the stars.

10

Pearl paced back and forth.

Madric emerged from the Sivan caravan waiting just inside the mammoth east gate and went over to Pearl. "My dear, you are wearing a hole in the road."

Pearl hissed, "Where is that boy?"

"We must leave now."

"We can't leave the boy in this place. It is soon to go up in flames."

"Regardless, the caravan must leave immediately. You must understand that we are putting the lives of others at risk if we tarry any longer."

Pearl grabbed Madric's hand. "Please. Just a few more minutes."

"No. We must go!"

Madric and Pearl swiveled to the sound of soldiers' leather boots slapping the stone streets. They looked at each other, realizing soldiers were advancing upon the gate.

Others heard the sound too, and rushed the gate, trying to get out and creating a bottleneck. A great wail poured from the people, and the bellowing from frightened pack animals only created more confusion. The throng turned on itself, beating and shoving those in front to the ground. Many people fell and were trampled.

Alarmed, the Sivan leader gave the signal to exit the city. With their beasts laden with goods, they pushed through the crowd, sometimes knocking terrified civilians down under the sharp hooves of their borax.

Pearl and Madric ran to take their place in the caravan, which was now moving forward at a fast pace. Others rushed behind the caravan, as it was moving past the cluster of people fighting among themselves to press through the gate.

Pearl heard her name called and turned around, but was pushed forward by the horde behind her. She could only manage to raise one arm, frantically hoping whoever was calling would see her signaling.

Outside the gate, the caravan pushed onward, the leader determined to leave Bhuttanian territory as fast as possible. He knew the Blue Queen's scouts were stationed out of sight beyond the knolls northeast, watching the mayhem, but he was confident they would not interfere with his people, since Siva was an ally.

Seeing the Sivan leader was determined to leave the city, Pearl dropped out of the caravan and clung to the side of the city's wall.

A platoon of soldiers arrived at the gate and immediately commandeered the gatehouse, which housed the winches and pulleys for the portcullis.

Bhuttanian civilians, frantic to get their families out at all costs, confronted the soldiers by throwing rocks and debris at them.

Angry at the pathetic assault by the ragtag mob, the soldiers made quick work of their attackers with sharp swords.

Fleeing families slipped on the blood from the dead and dying alike. Others stumbled over prone bodies while the soldiers battled to clear the street.

Barely audible above the din, Pearl heard her name again. She scanned the mass of people coming her way and thought she spotted Akela. "HURRY!" she cried, knowing he would never be able to hear over the noisy bedlam. She waved her arms frantically. "Hurry, little one," she mumbled to herself.

The soldiers, now in charge of the gatehouse, began turning the wheel controlling the massive portcullis.

Nearly trampled by the mob spilling forth, Pearl

held her ground at the very edge of the gate until the sharpened spikes of the portcullis were almost touching the street.

A small figure shot through, but his robe caught on one of the iron prongs before it clanged shut against the stone pavement.

Akela, thrown to the ground, reached back to pull his robe from the massive iron prong, but it wouldn't tear.

A soldier, angry because he had been hit several times with rubble, approached the boy frantically trying to pull his robe from the gate. "You little whelp. You probably threw a rock at me. I'll show you!" he cried, poking his sword through the lattice grill of the portcullis.

Pearl jumped over Akela with a small knife and stabbed the soldier's forearm as it reached through the grill.

Shocked and wounded, the soldier dropped his sword.

Quickly seeing an opportunity, Pearl picked up his sword and, with one swoop, cut the Akela's robe free from the massive gate. Grabbing the boy, she threw him over her shoulder and ran. They had to make the safety of the caravan, or they would be picked off by soldiers on the ramparts now unleashing a rain of arrows on the fleeing populace, purely for sport.

Dodging arrows, Pearl ran in a zigzag pattern until she reached the caravan and put Akela on the back of the last borax in line. Exhausted, she grabbed the tail of the great beast and let it pull her along.

It wasn't long before Maura's soldiers intercepted the fleeing caravan, offering aid as they did to everyone escaping the city. The soldiers produced flasks of water and patties of fried bread while Hasan Daegian healers treated the wounded before the refugees were sent to a camp where they would be safe from the fighting.

After gratefully accepting the bread and water, Pearl rested against the borax, weeping. Weary from months of anxiety, her mind gave way to blind panic. Not only did she not know if KiKu and Timon had accomplished their mission, but she still had to answer to Maura, regardless of the outcome. It wouldn't be long before the Blue Queen's soldiers realized who she was and came for her, along with the rest of KiKu's wives.

"Mistress Pearl," said a timid voice. "Would you like my bread? It's sweet with honey in it." A small hand patted her head. "Are you crying because I was late? There were so many people coming out of their houses. And there were gangs of rowdy boys attacking people and stealing their things. It took me much time to get past them unnoticed. Please don't cry."

Pearl opened her weeping eyes to see Akela was offering his crumbling morsel of bread to her.

Wiping the tears from her cheeks, she said, "I'm not angry with you, Akela. I'm angry at life. I'm angry at what the world has become. Eat your bread. You must be hungry."

Akela nodded and happily stuffed the bread into his mouth. He had discarded his robe and was clothed only in a filthy loincloth and dusty sandals.

Pearl smiled, watching him eat with such relish. She noticed Akela had grown since he joined their little troop, and wondered if he would live long enough to reach manhood, but at the moment he was still a little boy, greedily eating his fried honey bread and smacking his lips.

Picking up her water and bread ration from the ground where she had dropped it, she took a long drink from the earthenware flask.

"Aren't you going to eat your bread?" asked Akela.

"No, and neither are you. It's been on the ground."

Akela looked at Pearl in dismay. "Waste of food."

Pearl hailed a soldier carrying a basket of bread and plucked three large patties from it. She tossed one to Akela. "There now—another one for you, and two for me. That should fill you up until we get a proper meal."

"What about the one that fell on the ground?"

Pearl laughed. "You are such a greedy little bugger. I'm sure this borax, which has kindly loaned her back and her tail, wouldn't mind if a honey bread has fallen on the ground." She went in front of the borax, which sniffed at the bread and, with a massive tongue, swept it out of her hand.

Akela patted the borax's neck. "He likes it."

"She likes it," corrected Pearl. For a few seconds Pearl forgot about the war, Maura, and even KiKu, but that was dashed when she saw four Hasan Daegian soldiers with a lieutenant approaching.

"And so the last leg of our journey begins," she mumbled.

Akela followed her gaze and, seeing the soldiers, jumped off the borax, melting into the crowd milling around the caravan.

Pearl watched Akela disappear. "If I survive this, I'll find you, little Akela. I swear I will." Bravely, she turned to face the soldiers, who had already collected Madric and Tippu. She fell into step with them. There was no use resisting. The three women clasped hands, wondering what fate awaited them.

11

Maura entered the tent stealthily.

Most of the generals did not even realize she was standing in a corner listening to them discuss tomorrow's campaign. Only when a servant lit the lamps did Alexanee catch a glimpse of blue in the shadows. He immediately gave the Bhuttanian salute.

The other generals followed his gaze and followed suit, each one trying to remember if they had said anything to displease the empress.

Maura was not known for a forgiving disposition. And she was pleased that her generals feared her, which made them easier to control. She knew their hatred of her, since she had placed spies in their tents who repeated every word of treason. As long as they did her bidding, Maura didn't care how they felt about her. Giving them a slight nod, she strolled over to study the map they were perusing. "So, my fine generals, can we take Bhuttani with a minimum of bloodshed?"

"It is doubtful," remarked Alexanee, looking at the other generals to support him.

"Why say you thus?"

No one answered straightaway, and the generals avoided eye contact. A grizzled old general with gray hair braided down his back finally replied, "They will fight to the death. We Bhuttanians are bred for war. It is all we have ever known."

Maura sighed. "Then position our catapults where the city will have an ample view of them."

"Yes, Great Mother," they murmured.

"Any word from Cappet?" Maura asked.

Alexanee shook his head. "We know there have been riots in the streets, which Jezra's soldiers have put down. I hear they are killing civilians for sport."

"All the more reason to convince the populace to support us," responded Maura.

"I do not wish to be disrespectful, but that is not the Bhuttanian way," Alexanee countered. "We expect our soldiers to be brutal at the outset of a battle. The people should not have gone out into the streets."

"I see," Maura said, pondering the cruelty of the people she wished to conquer. Would they ever accept her as ruler, or would she have to utterly crush them for the survivors to obey? She was tired of the war, tired of the killing, tired of the intrigue, but it was almost over. Win or lose, tomorrow it would be over. She would either be the victor or the vanquished, but it would be finished.

Maura turned again to study the map. "What of the Dinii? Have they made contact?" she asked.

The generals looked to Alexanee to answer. Frankly, they disliked speaking to Maura directly. She gave them pause, since many of their comrades' bones had been fused to the Aga's horrid throne. They did not want their bones to be added as well.

Alexanee rubbed his chin with his thumb. "We have not seen them, but have deposited raw meat as well as live animals in the forest east of the city, as you request-ed, and they were all gone in the morning."

Maura gave a ghost of a smile. "Did you leave ale as well?"

"Yes, Great Mother," several of the generals said together.

"And it was gone as well?"

They nodded.

"Then they are here."

"How can we be sure?" asked Alexanee.

"Because they suspect Empress Gitar might be here," Maura replied.

One general, whose face bore an ugly scar from a sword across his face, asked, "But shouldn't we consult with them about tomorrow?"

Maura shrugged. "There's nothing to discuss. Chaun Maaun has sworn a blood oath to exact revenge for the death of his sisters and the destruction of the City of the Peaks. He will help us if he so chooses—or not.

"Even if there is not a battle, and the Dinii wish to rain retribution upon the city by killing every man, woman, and child they find, we will not interfere. Not a single Dini shall be harmed—upon pain of death."

The generals looked at each other in disbelief.

Stunned, Alexanee blustered, "Surely, Great Mother, you are not going to give carte blanch to these savage animals."

Maura slammed her fist on the table, on top of the battle maps. "YOU DARE TO CALL THE DINII ANIMALS AFTER YOU HAVE NEARLY BROUGHT THE WORLD TO ITS KNEES?"

The generals drew back at Maura's anger. Many put their hands on the hilts of their swords.

Maura confronted them. "The world is changing, my fine generals, and we must change with it. Either Bhuttani surrenders tomorrow, or it will be ground into dust like Anqara."

"But our homes—our families," protested several of

the generals.

"For those who still had kith in Bhuttani, you were told to send word advising your families to leave. At this very moment, Hasan Daegian soldiers are meeting those who left by the east gate and taking the refugees to a safe place, away from the fighting. Couriers will bring word of your families as soon as they can. Don't worry. We are providing food, water, and tents for their comfort. If they haven't left as ordered, then they will be considered traitors."

"But the Dinii?"

"As you know the Bhuttanian mindset, I know the Dinii. They will not harm those in the refugee camp."

Several generals gave sighs of relief, though others understood the implications of Maura's rounding up their families and placing them in a camp. She was holding them hostage. No doubt they would be put to death if the generals did not obey her.

Obviously, Maura had doubts about the Bhuttanian generals waging war against their capital city. While they admired her cunning, they were distraught to see their culture, as they had known it, coming to an end. The absolute rule of Bhuttan was broken, and the dream of a world empire given up as sand pouring through one's fingers.

Maura gave a ghost of a smile when she saw it dawn

on the generals that by rescuing their families she had made prisoners of them. She had come to despise the Bhuttanian generals for their hypocrisy. They worried about their kinsmen, and wanted Maura to grant mercy to their families, yet it had never occurred to them to show the same pity for the Anqarians, Dinii, and Hasan Daegians they slaughtered. It was all Maura could do to mask her revulsion, for they must never know the depth of her hatred of them.

Alexanee looked at Maura in amazement. He had many spies at court, but they had failed to alert him to the refugee camp with only Hasan Daegian guards. He was glad his wife and child were awaiting him in his tent. However, Maura could have them put to death on a whim, any time she liked.

He hoped no idiot tried to assassinate Maura between now and the morning. Even if an assassin did manage to kill her, the Dinii, along with the Hasan Daegian and Anqarian soldiers, would exact a terrible price from the Bhuttanians.

Alexanee tried to rub away the throbbing in his forehead. The world had turned topsy-turvy. Tomorrow, a Hasan Daegian queen would sit upon the throne of the Great Aga. How had this come to pass?

Maura motioned for a servant to bring a lamp over to the table so she could examine the maps more clearly.

She pulled out a detailed map of Bhuttani and pointed at the west gate. "If Cappet does not open the gate at dawn, we can assume he is either dead or has struck a deal with Jezra. Either way, we will batter the city gate down with the catapults. I want to be riding through the streets by midmorning."

"Yes, Great Mother," murmured the generals.

"If any of you stumble upon Mikkotto Sumsumito-yo, bring her to me."

"What of Jezra and her son?" asked Alexanee. "After all, the boy is Aga Dorak's firstborn."

Maura was ready for this question. She understood the implications Alexanee was raising, and pointed a finger at the generals. "Let us remember Aga Dorak never made Jezra his princess royal or his empress. I was crowned empress, and I am his royal wife. My daughter, Princess Dyanna, is his legal heir. Jezra is to be considered his concubine, and any issue from that alliance to be of no consequence. My marriage and offspring take precedence over any other child conceived by Dorak. Also, I am the queen of Hasan Daeg and a royal. Nothing flows through Jezra's veins but that of a banker's brat who sold out his countrymen."

Alexanee broke the silence which followed Maura's declaration. He spoke calmly, trying to avoid a confrontation with Maura. "We do not question your right to rule as regent, but if something should happen to the princess, Jezra's son would be next in line to rule."

Maura leaned forward. "Are you suggesting Princess Dyanna's life may be in peril?"

"I am saying children become ill and die."

"My blood courses through her veins. Rest assured, my generals, she will not expire from illness, nor will she die from an accident. Princess Dyanna will sit upon the throne when she reaches the appropriate age."

"But when will that be? The women of the royal family of Hasan Daeg live a very long time."

"It will happen when it happens."

"But . . ." Alexanee could not finish his sentence because a courier entered the tent. She bowed and knelt before Maura, handing her a scroll.

Maura took the scroll and broke the seal. Leaning near a lamp, she read the names listed. Determined not to gloat, she threw the scroll onto the table. "Your families are safe and under the protection of the royal House de Magela. I must leave you good men now. I have much to prepare before dawn, as do you. Make sure everything is in order. I bid you good night."

The generals saluted her and fell to planning the assault for the morning. They dared not discuss their families or the Dinii, since many unseen ears might be listening to their conversation.

They knew in their hearts that Maura had bested them, and regardless of how they felt, at dawn they would fight their countrymen in order to put a small babe on the Bhuttanian throne lest their families be obliterated. They had no doubt Maura had given such orders to be enacted if they deserted to join the city's fighters.

Alexanee looked at the disgruntled officers surrounding the table. He picked up a piece of charcoal to mark the map. "We must hang together in this endeavor, my brothers, or tomorrow we shall all hang together from the battlements of Bhuttani. Let us begin."

The generals nodded and bent over the table to finalize the plans for the taking of Bhuttani.

12

T he priests prayed in the great hall.

"Any change?" asked Empress Gitar, coming up behind Iegani. She stood listening to the resonance of the priests' chants echoing off the vaulted ceiling.

Iegani shook his head. "They drone on and on in the same repetitive verses."

"What can they be about?"

"I don't know. It is some sort of ritual, but what for I do not know."

Empress Gitar looked forlorn as she and Iegani stood among the chanting priests, who were unaware of their presence. "I wish I knew what was going on in the outside world. Once in a while, I hear a priest whisper something about the Blue Queen, but then he is hushed up."

"I guess it is safe to assume he was talking about

Maura, so she is still alive."

"How long have we've been here? It seems like hours, but Zedek intimated that we've been here for years."

"I wouldn't trust anything that reptile said, my dear niece."

"People rush by as though they were buzzing insects. Only once in awhile do they slow down enough that we can understand what they're saying."

"As they are now?"

"Yes, as in now. I can understand them perfectly, and they are not blurry. Do you think the chanting is having an effect?"

"I hope so. They may be trying to open a portal."

"In that case, we must gather the others and be ready. Where is Dorak?"

"The last I saw of him, he went to find Zedek."

"He should be with us."

"Not that we don't trust him," both Empress Gitar and Iegani said at the same moment, then looked at each and chuckled.

Empress Gitar declared, "It is good we can find some humor in this situation, but I should find Dorak."

Iegani reached out and grabbed Gitar's arm. "No, my dear. You must stay with me. Let us gather our people, and if there is a chance for freedom, we will make the transition together. Dorak is not our concern."

He sent a telepathic message to all the Dinii trapped in the netherworld.

One by one, they found their way to Gitar and Iegani.

13

KiKu's wives stood trembling in a little knot.

They had been summoned to the antechamber of Maura's tent. Their guard escort stood beside them impassively, never moving or responding to any of their questions.

The women waited nervously while they watched couriers and scribes bustle in and out of the main chamber. At one point the Royal Counsel Rubank was brought out in a palanquin, looking peevish, with a servant trying to mop the counsel's brow while shuffling alongside.

Madric said, "No matter what, we must not show fear."

The other women nodded but had little resolve. They were terrified.

A Hasan Daegian officer parted the thick curtains that divided the room and beckoned to the women. Their guards moved forward, so the women shuffled with them.

Once inside the main chamber of Maura's tent, the women spied the Blue Queen occupying the throne of bones perched upon an elevated dais with the uultepes lounging beside her. Maura was arrayed in the State Robe of the Aga, a stunning red and golden cape with embossed dragons. To signify the dual nature of her rule, she held the Royal Fan of the Hasan Daegians.

The darkened room was illuminated only by a few lamps, which filled the air with smoke.

The women let out a small gasp in unison. In the dark, chilly room, the hostages could see rays of bright light emitting from Maura's fingers and head. They knew Maura radiated an aura, but they had never seen her shimmer so. It only served to heighten their collective apprehension.

The guards about-faced abruptly and left the room.

Finding themselves directly before the Maura, the women spontaneously kowtowed, pressing their foreheads on the carpeted floor.

"Arise," they heard Maura say.

The women quickly stood and glanced about them. Near the empress stood Noabini, the High Priestess from the House of Magi, in her blue and green robes.

Madric felt her legs tremble and feared she was going to faint, but she had to stay strong. As KiKu's first wife, she must speak for the rest of the harem. She bowed and said, "Great Mother, we offer you greetings on this auspicious day."

Maura snapped her fan open and kept her eyes riveted on Madric. "Bring in Tippa."

A curtain to the right opened, and Tippa was escorted into the room.

Maura pointed her fan at Tippa. "Join them."

Tippa lit up with joy at seeing her sister-wives and ran to them.

The women forgot protocol and hugged each other fiercely, kissing each other's cheeks.

"Enough," ordered Maura, closing her fan with a loud clap.

The women instantly obeyed, bowing their heads. Tippu grabbed Tippa's hand, not letting go.

"Madric, will you speak?" asked Maura, looking intently at them.

"Yes, Great Mother, I can, but it would be best if Pearl answers your questions," replied Madric, hoping her voice did not quiver.

"Very well," replied Maura, standing. "Follow me."

The uultepes immediately rose. They passed near the

women with their snouts grazing the women's clothing, inhaling deeply.

Madric and Pearl dared not move, fearing any sudden movement might cause the great cats to attack. Tippa and Tippu clutched each other, closing their eyes as the beasts passed.

"Come, come," encouraged Maura. "My darlings won't hurt you."

Pearl gave a reassuring look to her companions and followed Maura into an adjoining chamber. Her natural curiosity overrode her anxiety, and she wondered how many rooms the tent held.

"You are Pearl, are you not?"

Startled, Pearl came to attention. "Yes, Great Mother," she replied, realizing they were in Maura's bedchamber. She watched young Hasan Daegian males remove the official robes and headdress until Maura was clothed in only a simple linen shift.

The room was well lit, so Pearl could no longer see light emanating from Maura, which helped her to relax a bit.

Maura sat in a chair, allowing her attendants to minister to her. They brought hot water for her feet to soak in and trays of food.

She motioned for the servants to bring chairs for the women, ignoring their looks of surprise. Maura rarely let anyone sit in her presence unless it was at a state banquet. Otherwise, her subordinates kowtowed in her presence. Generals and nobility stood. Only her personal favorites were allowed to sit before her.

The servants set up small tables beside the women and placed trays of food on them.

Maura ordered, "Bring my guests some colla tea," while studying the frazzled wives of KiKu.

"Does this mean you are not going to kill us?" asked Tippu, her eyes widening at the courteous treatment.

Pearl looked skeptically at the trays laden with tasty tidbits and wondered if the food was poisoned.

As if reading Pearl's mind, Maura laughed and asked for a plate to be given to the suspicious woman. "Would you be kind enough to select a few morsels for me," she instructed.

Pearl selected food from several trays with a utensil she was given and handed the plate to one of the male servants who served the empress.

He took the plate to Maura, who casually ate from the plate while observing Pearl. She could tell Pearl was still not convinced.

"Mistress Pearl, I assure you the food is not poisoned. I have never used poison to kill anyone. I hang them or kill them personally with my sword. If I were to have you killed, that would be the way."

"Are you going to hang us?" Tippu's voice wobbled.

Madric whispered, "Hush!"

Several of the servants giggled.

"You are a brave little bird," remarked Maura, looking amused. She took a sip of the colla tea. "Not at the moment, but I do have some questions."

Tippu gulped and bowed her head.

Feeling relieved, Pearl partook of food and accepted a cup of colla tea. The other women followed suit.

"Yes, Great Mother," replied Madric. "We shall answer to the best of our ability."

Maura asked, "Where is the little boy, Akela?"

Pearl swallowed before answering. "He ran away when he saw your guards coming for me."

"Do you know where he might be?"

"No, Great Mother, but he would not be far from food, so he is probably near the refugee camp."

Maura beckoned to a guard and whispered in her ear, causing the guard to leave the room quickly. The empress turned her attention back to the women. "Did KiKu and Timon receive my instructions?"

Pearl nodded. "Yes, Great Mother. Akela told me he found KiKu and relayed the message about the amulet."

"So you did not speak to KiKu yourself?"

"No, Great Mother. None of us have seen KiKu since he entered the temple. Akela has been the go-between for us. I can tell you this. Akela told me that before he left the temple to join us, he found KiKu locked in the cellar trussed up in a shroud."

"What about Timon?"

"Akela never saw Timon," Pearl replied, using the informal use of Timon's name since Maura was doing so.

"Did KiKu give Akela any information regarding Timon or their mission?"

Pearl bowed her head, afraid to look at Maura when giving her answer. "No, Great Mother."

The rest of the women paused in their eating and drinking, looking in alarm at Maura, who rose suddenly.

Tippu began to cry.

"Someone quiet that silly girl."

Tippa reached over and pinched Tippu, which only made the exhausted girl cry harder.

For once Pearl saw compassion in Maura's eyes.

Maura spoke kindly to Tippu, "Little one, I am not going to hang you. I can see all of you have lost much weight and have a haunted look about you. Your clothes are rags, and not fit for the wives of Prince KiKu. The mission has been a terrible burden. This is evident to all who look upon you."

Smiling, Maura continued, "You will be given a tent of your own with guards, so you need not fear retribution from anyone. Meals will be provided by my private chef, and you will be attended by the Royal Healer if you so desire. If the battle tomorrow is won, you will be sent home with all honors. Whether Prince KiKu and Prince Bes Amon Ptah have succeeded or not is no longer your concern. You have done your part. You may leave now with my blessing."

A servant motioned for the women to rise.

After giving a deep bow, the women began to back out of the tent. Suddenly Pearl looked up and spoke. "Great Mother?"

The servants gasped at the impropriety of Pearl speaking when not spoken to by the empress.

Maura motioned them to be quiet. "Yes, Lady Pearl."

"When next we meet, I will be bowing to you in the Imperial Court of the Agas. May the gods protect you from all harm tomorrow." Pearl bowed again and backed out of the room, aided by one of the male servants who attended the empress. She wished with all her heart that Maura would succeed in her quest.

The capture of Bhuttani would mean life for them all.

14

Mikkotto reviewed the troops.

She inspected repair work for the walls and food silos, giving orders that any looter was to be killed on sight. All gates to the city had been shut for hours and reinforced. Anyone trying to climb the walls to escape fell to their death with an arrow in their back.

Water was Mikkotto's principal concern, and she stationed guards by wells, including stockpiling the precious liquid in barrels near important buildings and squads of soldiers. The last thing she needed were guards leaving their posts to drink. Water boys made the rounds of each guard post every half hour with fresh water.

For days, all households had been encouraged to store as much water as possible, and the people obeyed by filling every bucket, vase, goblet, and cup at their disposal.

All fires were extinguished, except those of black-smiths who were still fashioning weapons.

The city residents, including the soldiers, had to eat cold rations. Even torches, lamps, and candles were snuffed out on the streets.

If Maura chose to attack in the darkness of night, Mikkotto didn't want to give her an advantage with flickering pinpoints of light emanating from the city.

Exhausted, Mikkotto returned to the palace, eating a quick meal of fruit and cheese while poring over detailed maps of the city. Her chamber was flooded with candlelight since dark curtains covered all the windows.

A doctor stood by, infusing a mild stimulant into a special drink for her.

Mikkotto quickly drank the concoction. "By the grace of Mekonia, this stuff is evil." She threw the goblet against the wall in disgust, but couldn't deny she was feeling refreshed. "Prepare me another one," she ordered the healer.

"Shouldn't you be out on the parapets?"

Mikkotto swung around with her hand on a dagger hidden in her shirtsleeve. "I just came from there," she answered Jezra.

"Are we ready?" asked Jezra, framed by the door wearing a stunning orange dress with golden silk flowers encircling the bodice and a gold tiara crowning her flaxen hair.

As always, Mikkotto was struck by her beauty. "As ready as we can be. The question is—if Maura attacks, will our soldiers fire arrows at their fathers and brothers?"

"Did you not hear what happened at the east gate? The soldiers fired upon those fleeing the city, killing hundreds."

"Why would they do such a thing?"

Jezra laughed. "For sport. What else?"

Mikkotto frowned. After the war, the city would need to rebuild its population again. She considered killing civilians for fun a wasteful squandering of their workforce. "I hope those idiots recovered all the arrows. They are very valuable."

"I received a report that the soldiers opened the gate one last time, recovering the arrows and stripping the bodies of anything valuable before returning behind the walls."

"Did they dispose of the bodies?"

Jezra shook her head.

"Wonderful. Now we have rotting corpses stinking up the east gate."

"What does it matter? When Maura finally strikes, there will be thousands of putrid corpses decaying in the sun," Jezra replied with a sardonic smile.

"It does matter if the city is sieged for a long period. Those corpses could cause an epidemic among the people."

Jezra shrugged while biting into a fruit.

Mikkotto shook her head. "I guess it never occurred to you that there is a slight possibility we may have to flee on horseback. How can horses gallop on a road strewn with decomposing bodies?"

Jezra maintained her nonchalant air. "Regardless of what happens, my son and I will not be leaving this palace."

"You say that now."

Jezra drifted from the room, the train of her stiff gown raking across the stone floor as she muttered, "I will never flee. Never. Never. Never."

Mikkotto watched her leave, firm in her resolve to kill Jezra at the first opportunity and install her son on the throne, to be overseen by a puppet vizier of Mikkotto's choosing while she went back to Hasan Daeg, triumphant as queen.

Yes, at the first opportunity.

15

Maura shunned heavy metal armor.

Instead, she selected a light suit of borax leather. She did wear a metal brace about her neck, knowing that's where her opponents would strike first, since nothing else had killed her thus far.

Stepping outside her tent, she gazed at the heavens. The night sky was at its darkest, but Maura knew it would be dawn soon.

A groom held the reins of Dorak's ebony warhorse while Maura checked the saddle and bridle.

KiKu had related the story of how he cut the girth on Zoar's saddle, causing a serious injury when Zoar fell off the horse.

Now Maura always checked her saddle before mounting. Not that a fall would really hurt her, but a poisoned blade inserted somewhere in the seams of the saddle might slow her down. Sooner or later, someone would discover a poison to which even she would succumb.

Everything seemed in order. She jumped on the spirited horse and pulled the reins out of the groom's hands. As Maura rode through the camp with the uultepes loping behind, Hasan Daegian and Anqarians cheered. The Bhuttanians remained silent, watching her ride past. Nevertheless, they went about the business of making ready for battle, checking their weapons, donning their armor, and stuffing food rations about their persons. Who knew how long it might be before they had a proper meal again?

All the soldiers looked up as a thin ray of light struggled over a distant mountain. Fighting would begin soon.

Maura rode to a steep slope which gave way to a broad plain leading to the city. There were no trees, no vegetation of any kind to impede her army's progress as they advanced upon to Bhuttani—just a desert-looking plain rutted by wagon wheels, animal hooves, and the myriad of footprints made by travelers over the decades.

To the north flowed a river where Bhuttani got most of its drinking water, but it was not like the clear, sweet, sparkling water of Hasan Daeg. It was brown and sluggish like the land surrounding it.

Coming upon a small knot of generals making final preparations, Maura stopped her warhorse and observed her officers, composed of some Hasan Daegians and Anqarians, but mostly Bhuttanians.

She studied them closely. Their armor and horses were decorated with the insignias of their rank and station, but it was the Bhuttanians who stood out, with colorful plumes in their massive helmets and gleaming armor with scarlet cloth showing through the gaps in their shoulder pauldrons.

They bowed their heads and gave the Bhuttanian salute.

"Is everything in place?"

"Yes, Great Mother," they answered in unison.

"Communication established?"

"We have both runners and riders, plus soldiers planted on the hills with signal flags and fire," answered Alexanee.

Maura grunted.

The Bhuttanians grunted as well.

"Then let us proceed. May your gods protect and favor us with a decisive win, with as little death and destruction as possible. Remember, our goal is to capture the city, not obliterate it." Maura turned her horse around, knowing this was an opportune moment for an assassin to strike.

Alexanee pulled his horse alongside her as the others left for their assigned positions.

Maura looked sideways at him, especially the placement of his hands. They were on the reins of his horse, not clutching a dirk.

Maura relaxed. "So it begins, General Alexanee."

"So it does, Great Mother."

"Let's hope your death god Bhuttu slumbers and is not reveling at the prospect of blood being spilled throughout the city."

"I am hoping Jezra will come to her senses and open the gates, sparing the city, if only for the sake of the people still inside the walls."

"You almost make me laugh, General. Do you remember Jezra as being a compassionate and intelligent woman? Even if she wanted to, Mikkotto would never permit it. There is nothing waiting for Mikkotto except a hangman's noose, so she will fight to the death."

"Then I will make it my goal to find her and kill her."

"Only if you have to. I want her taken alive if possible."

"As you wish, Great Mother." Alexanee paused for a moment, wondering if he should ask the next question. "We still have not established contact with Chaun Maaun. Have you had any word?"

"You must trust me in this, General. They will show themselves at a moment of their choosing. They are no doubt watching us at this very moment."

Alexanee swiveled in his saddle. He did not like the thought of the Dinii behind or above him. He had learned to respect their abilities and greatly admired what they had accomplished at Anqara. They had saved an entire civilization almost single-handedly. He had also learned to fear them.

"They are here, even if soaring above the clouds," Maura commented.

A servant rushed to take the reins of Maura's warhorse, which was pawing the ground in nervous anticipation.

Maura jumped off and strode over to the massive royal wagon upon which the throne of bones had been installed again, but the top had been taken off this time so all could clearly see Maura.

With a quick leap, she was on the wagon and allowing her servants to adorn her in Zoar's magnificent robes—the very ones he wore when ordering the city of Anqara to surrender.

Alexanee's brow furrowed.

"You disapprove, General?" asked Maura, studying his face. "You think it is pouring salt into a wound?"

"It's uncommon for you to make such a symbolic statement."

"Are these not the Official Robes of the Aga? Should the citizens of Bhuttani not see that I occupy the position of the aga? Symbolic—yes. Rubbing the Bhuttanian nose in it—perhaps. Stating my claim to rule—absolutely!"

Not wishing to argue with Maura, Alexanee looked at the sky. "Daylight approaches. We must proceed posthaste."

Maura sat on the throne holding the Royal Fan of Hasan Daeg and the ancient Sword of the Agas. Below the dais was an array of goods from all the lands where Maura had established order—precious metals, beautiful bolts of cloth, medicines, plants, tools, cookware, pottery, bags of seeds, shoes, leather goods, jewelry— anything a heart could desire. And they were all things the Bhuttanians needed, since Maura had cut off much of the trade to the city for years.

Taking a deep breath, Maura composed herself and snapped her fan open, giving the signal for soldiers to coax the borax forward. With each lumbering plod of the borax, Maura was moving closer to the true test of her leadership.

By the time the sun sank behind the distant mountains, Maura would either be the Regent Aga, or she would be dead.

16

Timon gnawed on a leaf.

He felt strength leaving him in the hours it had taken him to make his way to the temple. He constantly had to evade patrols, which were interrogating anyone they found in the street as possible saboteurs. The soldiers' methods of questioning were quite brutal, and after stealing everything of value, they left the poor, battered soul lying in the street. Hiding behind some barrels, Timon leaned against a wall, breathing heavily, but feeling new strength surging through his veins as he chewed the pungent leaf. He looked at the sky. It was getting light. Dawn couldn't be far off. Timon had to hurry to the temple, or he would be caught by soldiers sooner or later.

Renewed by the energizing tonic of the leaf, Timon rose to his feet and crept stealthily from doorway to doorway, as KiKu had shown him, until he realized he could see the massive doors of the temple's entrance. All he had to do was step out of the shadows and cross a courtyard, passing the fountain to enter by way of the cellar door on the far side of the building.

Timon looked both ways and listened intently. He saw no one and heard nothing, but he did not budge, for it was light enough that anyone could spot him. Still, he had to move, and move now. Gathering his courage, he emerged from the darkness of a recessed doorway and began across the square when a trio of soldiers stumbled into the courtyard from a narrow side street.

"Hey, you there. Halt!" cried a soldier.

Timon stopped in a blind panic and stared at them. *What am I doing?* Pulling up his robe, Timon turned and ran as fast as he could, with the soldiers hard behind him. He hurried into the alley where the cellar entrance was and pushed against it, looking behind him.

The door stood fast.

Timon pushed again.

The ancient door didn't yield.

Timon looked to his right.

The soldiers were almost upon him.

With all his might, Timon reared up and gave the door a ferocious kick. The door gave way. Timon fell into the blackness of the entryway and slammed the door shut behind him. Leaning against it, he listened. Above his rapid heartbeat, he heard the soldiers muttering.

"Let's be gone. If that lad wants to enter the temple of Bhuttu, he's welcome to it."

Another soldier with a high-pitched voice concurred. "He's no threat. Probably wants to sacrifice himself to Bhuttu to save his family. Poor bastard. Yes, let's be off."

Expelling a sigh of relief, Timon listened until he was sure the soldiers were gone, and then rolled barrels up against the door in case they had a change of heart.

Now Timon had to finish his mission. He must find the amulet and release the Dinii. Betting that Hilkiah would be in the ceremonial hall, Timon made his way through the secret passageways, his breathing becoming more and more labored. Once he stopped and leaned against a wall made slimy by the constant seeping of water and pressed his hand against his chest. His heart was beating so hard, Timon thought it might explode.

Taking another leaf out of his pocket, he chewed it and immediately felt better, but was becoming aware of the awful toll the stimulant was taking on his body. He realized the healer's warning was true. The herb was giving him immediate strength, but ultimately weakening his heart.

Timon finished chewing and swallowed the awful-tasting leaf before continuing to make his way to the great chamber, where he knew all the priests and the novitiates would be praying for a decisive Bhuttanian victory.

He fervently hoped Maura would tear down the temple stone by stone once she had conquered the city. He hated the god Bhuttu and everything the cult of death stood for.

Hearing faint chanting in the distance, Timon stepped up his pace, still pondering what he would do once he found his way to the great hall.

Hilkiah, though a doughy fop, was a big man, and would not give up the amulet easily, and Timon doubted he had the strength to overcome him. He had to find a weapon. Timon smiled at the thought of killing Hilkiah. It would be one evil deed Timon would be only too glad to perform.

17

Alexanee waved a red flag.

Thousands of soldiers from every corner of the empire, stepped out onto the dry, sandy plain and beat their shields with swords, creating a great sound which thundered across the plain.

Those inside the city walls, Bhuttanian soldiers and citizens alike, rushed to the battlements and rooftops to gaze upon enemy soldiers marching in lockstep as they encircled the city.

Frantic women screamed while gathering their babes. Men gaped in horror at the terrifying sight, clasping their hands over their ears to drown out the sound.

Never before had Bhuttan experienced war within its borders, and the people were horrified. The populace now realized the raw terror others had felt at the hand of Bhuttan's powerful army as it swept across the world, destroying all in its path. Many threw themselves down to pray, fearing the wrath of the many foreign gods they had offended, for now the revengeful hand of those gods was upon them.

Bhuttanian soldiers turned to each other and asked, "Are our brothers really about to storm the city? Has that blue witch sowed hatred in their warriors' hearts?"

Mikkotto stood upon a platform high above the troops with Jezra and her son. "Steady, men!" she called out. "This is all for show. Your real queen stands before you with Dorak's son and heir. Remember your blood oaths. Remember who the real aga is!"

Soldiers murmured amongst themselves. "Yes, Dorak's son is the real aga. Surely our generals serving the witch will realize this. They will turn against the Blue Queen before they reach the gate. It's all a ploy to lure the pretender closer to the city."

"Have the boy wave to the people," muttered Mikkotto to Jezra.

Jezra stood transfixed, watching Maura's army march closer and closer, still beating their shields.

"JEZRA!"

Trembling, Jezra pushed the boy forward, but he cried out and ran under his mother's skirts.

A murmur of disquiet rose from the people.

Mikkotto reached down, grabbing the little boy and

shoving him in front of her. She whispered into his ear, "Wave, or I swear I shall bite off one of your ears and swallow it whole."

Eyes closed, the boy did as commanded, prodded by Mikkotto's dagger pressing against his bony spine.

Jezra stepped forward and clasped her son's hand while managing a false smile and waving too.

Heartened by this display of solidarity, the city's soldiers rattled their shields as well, and yelled taunts.

Seeing the people's spirit revitalized, Mikkotto gave the signal for Jezra to depart. She barked at Jezra's guards, "Take the aga and the aganess back to the palace and guard them with your lives. That boy must survive at all costs."

Jezra shot Mikkotto a grateful look. She was glad to get away from the noise and the stench. Safe in the Imperial Palace, she would distract her son until the battle was over and the danger had passed. Since the palace was in the middle of the city, they might not even hear the fighting. The thought gave Jezra comfort. She had never experienced a battle, and she didn't want to experience one now.

When the Bhuttanians seized Anqara, she had already been married to Dorak and far from harm's way. As she was hurrying down the steps to her palanquin, it never occurred to her that Maura might capture the city.

Not once.

18

The refugees heard the clamor.

Throwing down their bowls of gruel, they dashed about in panic, thinking Maura's army was coming to kill them. Many climbed into trees to look across the plain on which Bhuttani sat.

Akela was one of them. He scampered up a tree and climbed to its highest branch. Straining his eyes to see the drama unfold, Akela was grateful the camp was on a knoll at the edge of a small forest, which an ancient aga had planted for his pleasure many miles from the city.

Akela could not make out details, and could only discern a broad outline of what was taking place before him.

Pointing, he cried, "The Blue Queen's army is descending upon the city!"

"How many soldiers does that bitch have?" asked an

old fighter, retired due to a bad leg.

Akela did not know the exact number of soldiers in the Blue Queen's army, but knew they were many. "More soldiers than there are stars in the heavens," he replied, upon which the old fighter grunted and hurried to his tent to collect his sword. Maybe the gods would be kind and let him die in battle. He was determined to make his way back to the city to fight, even if he had to crawl.

"What else, boy?" a woman cried, wondering if her son was still alive and marching in the service of that blue devil. If it was true, she doubted that she would be able to withstand the shame.

"I see a huge platform pulled by many borax. It is tall as any mountain. The soldiers are parting to make way for the platform, but it is moving very slowly."

"That must be her," cried a young mother who was suckling her baby.

Another woman replied, "Yes, the Blue Queen will demand that the city surrender. Perhaps those left behind the city's walls should yield. I have never seen such might."

Startled at the woman's defeatist statement, the man standing next to her spat at her feet and turned his back.

Unnerved by the man's contemptuous response, the woman said, "If our defeat was not possible, why are we hiding in the woods like frightened animals and eating morsels of food thrown to us by our enemies?"

Many nodded their heads in agreement.

Fearful of retaliation, many fled deeper into the woods, running past the fierce female Hasan Daegian soldiers who stepped quickly out of their way.

One of the soldiers remarked, "They'll be back when they get hungry."

"Or to slit our throats while we sleep," replied a second in command.

"Then we shan't sleep," murmured her comrade, standing on her tiptoes to see the spectacle unfolding on the plain.

"We shall have to round them up later," complained the Hasan Daeg soldier.

The commander-in-charge agreed. "Yes, we will, but right now we have orders to find this Akela lad. The other guards can round up the refugees and put them back in the camp." She looked up into the trees and pointed. "That small boy up in the very top of the tree. He fits the description. Maybe this is our lucky day, and he's the boy our queen wants."

Another soldier stepped in front of her commander, blocking the way. "Let us wait until the boy tires and comes down of his own accord. Otherwise, we will have to cut the tree down. No one willingly goes to see our queen when summoned."

Her superior nodded, "Wise counsel. We will grab the boy as soon as he comes down, but do it quietly. We don't want the others to see us and possibly attack, trying to save him."

The soldier grunted in reply—a Bhuttanian custom the Hasan Daegians had acquired.

They did not have long to wait.

Akela heard a small rustle and felt a rush of wind behind him and looked over his shoulder. To his great surprise, Akela saw many gigantic beings with faces and torsos like humans, but clothed with feathers and sprouting great wings high in the trees behind him. Crying out in fear, Akela loosened his grip and fell from the tree. He tried unsuccessfully to grab onto branches as he plummeted, only to be snatched from certain death at the last moment by a great, clawed talon.

Akela found himself face-to-face with one of the strange creatures, whose face was grinning at him. He pummeled this strange being with his fists, fearing he was about to be eaten.

The bird-woman swooped down and carefully dropped the boy into the arms of the waiting Hasan Daegian warriors, who did not seem to fear the bizarre beasts.

He heard one soldier speak in Anqara to the other.

"The Dinii are here. Nothing will stop us now."

THE DINII!

Akela had always heard vague rumors of the strange race of bird people, but thought them to be the tales old women concocted to frighten their grandchildren. He had also listened to KiKu and Timon whisper about the Dinii. That's what the fuss over the feather found in the temple was about!

One warrior threw Akela over her shoulder like a sack of Anqarian apples and carried him to a comrade waiting on a warhorse.

He was very confused, but then Akela was confused about everything that was happening, and yearned deeply for the comfort of Madric, Pearl, Tippa, and Tippu.

Fearing for his life, Akela squirmed in the warrior's grasp and managed to sink his teeth into her neck. Out of the corner of his eye, he saw another soldier on a nearby warhorse rear back to strike him.

That's when everything went black.

19

Maura sat atop her throne.

A team of lumbering, snorting borax pulled the great wagon that housed the hideous chair. Maura, wearing all the regalia denoting her station, was easily visible from a great distance.

Beside the rolling platform was a retinue of generals in her command, in full uniform noting their rank and country of origin, and riding spirited white warhorses. The Bhuttanian generals rode in front.

Behind walked major dignitaries from every country of the Bhuttanian Empire.

Mikkotto eyed this procession from a protected vantage point in a sentry tower. She had instructed archers not to shoot, as she knew Maura would stay out of range, and she did not want edgy soldiers to waste arrows. Metal was at a premium for the arrowheads, so much so that she had ordered more arrows made without metal tips, instead having their points hardened over a fire.

Watching the platform make its way to the west gate, Mikkotto had to admit Maura cast an imposing visage, sitting upright on a throne that barely swayed as it was pulled across the barren plain.

Mikkotto had to assume Maura's army had smoothed the well-traveled road to the west gate, filling in any dips or ruts to provide the platform with a smooth journey.

The line of soldiers encircling Bhuttani still banged on their shields. Only when the platform reached the circle did the soldiers on the west side open their line, letting the platform through and falling in step behind it.

It took an hour for Maura's regal procession to traverse the wide plain outside the city and come to a halt close enough to the city's wall for her to be heard.

By that time all rooftops, windows of high buildings, and battlements were filled with curious onlookers, many of them furious, some of them resigned, but most of them frightened. Never before had a foreign army breached their borders, much less threatened the capital.

It was not lost on many who had witnessed the fall of Anqara that Maura had donned the very same royal robes that Zoar wore when he demanded the city's surrender.

The platform halted, and a trumpet gave the signal for the others to stop as well. The beating of the shields ceased.

Nothing could be heard across the plain except for a harsh wind whistling through the battlements.

Each general turned his horse to form a single line comprised of twenty generals on each side of the platform.

Dignitaries who had been marching behind Maura now proceeded to the front of the platform. They bowed to Maura before forming a line, standing in front of the platform facing the city, each one brandishing the flag of their country or tribal alliance. There were nineteen flags fluttering in the hot wind. Soldiers closed ranks until there was one continuous line encircling the city.

Maura rose from the throne and stood ramrod straight, holding the Royal Fan of Hasan Daeg, denoting her position as queen of Hasan Daeg, and Zoar's sword for the authority of the aga. She held them both aloft and turned back and forth for everyone to see. "Citizens of Bhuttan, I am Maura de Magela, tenth queen of Hasan Daeg, the royal wife of Aga Dorak, Crowned Empress, and Regent Dowager for Dyanna, Crowned

Princess. I have come to install Princess Dyanna, blood daughter of Aga Dorak and granddaughter to Aga Zoar, as the legitimate heir of the Bhuttanian Empire.

"Open your gates and rejoice that the royal line of succession will be reestablished, and that I have led home your brothers, fathers, and sons."

"Your claim is a fraud!" cried Mikkotto. "The real heir, Dorak's firstborn, sits upon the throne."

If Maura was disturbed to hear Mikkotto's voice, she showed no sign up it. "You who presumes to address your empress, identify yourself."

Mikkotto shouted back, "You know well who I am. Where is Dorak, Maura? Where is the aga? It is known that you had him murdered." Ignoring her questions, Maura called out, "Why do you claim to speak for my people? You have no authority over them. You are a traitor and cast out from your own country. Now you bring treachery upon this city. You are an illegitimate pretender."

Mikkotto reared her head back and laughed. "As are you, Blue Witch. I serve Jezra, wife of Dorak and mother to his eldest son. Your bastard bitch cannot rule. Women have never ruled in Bhuttan."

"Then why are you shouting at me like a fishmonger's wife? Is there not a man with more authority over you who should be speaking? For as you just said, no woman has ever ruled in Bhuttan."

Maura pointed her fan at Mikkotto and addressed the anxious observers. "Do not listen to this woman. She will lead you down the path to perdition. We have come with food, provisions of every kind, including metal, medicine, and seeds. Your days of deprivation are over. Bhuttan can begin anew—a fresh start."

"Seeds?" shouted an old man standing in the rampart. "What would we do with seeds? War is all we have ever known. It is all we want."

Maura shouted, "I have brought you a bounty of good things. You can live without fear, and help to rebuild Kaseri!"

The old man answered, "We are warriors. We live without fear now."

"Do you? Look about the city. Soldiers from every country of the known world surround the Bhuttanian Empire. I control everything but this city." She pointed the Sword of the Aga at the Bhuttanian generals. "Even your mighty warriors know Bhuttan cannot go on as before.

"They will not fight us!" exclaimed the people.

"I give you one last chance. Open the gates, or the deaths that follow will be upon your heads."

"Maura, since you speak of heads, I have one for you." Mikkotto reared back and threw a severed head over the wall onto the ground, which gently rolled to a stop.

Four soldiers, using their shields to protect them from zinging arrows, ran and grabbed it.

Alexanee gestured to the soldier holding the head to bring it to him. He looked at it carefully and then signaled the soldier away before speaking to Maura. "It is Cappet. I'm sure of it. Jezra must have learned of our pact with him."

There was no more talking to be done. Bhuttani had sealed its fate.

Maura snapped her fan shut.

The pounding of large drums began.

Maura took off the robes, exposing her in full battle dress. One assistant placed a silver-plated helmet with the horns of a wild borax bull upon her head.

Thrusting her sword in the air, Maura nimbly jumped on the back of Dorak's ebony steed and galloped off.

Servants grabbed the halters of the borax and slowly turned them around to take them to the safety of a pasture several miles away from the fighting that would soon begin.

With the generals following, Maura rode around the city walls with her arm thrust upright, holding the Sword of the Aga so it glimmered in the morning light.

Many a Bhuttanian vainly shot arrows, but the generals and Maura were careful to stay out of range.

Once Maura had made a complete circle around the city, she and the generals separated, each one going to a separate division of warriors. The soldiers retreated as well, except for the teams of fifty arming the catapults with massive boulders.

Alexanee gave the signal to those manning the catapults to release the boulders, which flew high into the sky and slammed against the thick walls of Bhuttani. The sound was deafening as the ground shook.

People screamed, fleeing from the battlements amidst falling rock debris.

The war against Bhuttani had begun in earnest.

20

Akela blinked.

He was slung over a warhorse with his hands tied behind his back.

A blue hand grabbed his hair, lifting his head.

Akela looked up to see the Blue Queen staring down at him.

Maura's long blue-black hair blew in the wind beneath her battle helmet, which was adorned with great horns. The Blue Queen looked like an angry goddess unleashing her wrath upon the people.

Akela shuddered with fear at her imposing countenance. He was not prepared for the kind voice that greeted him.

"Boy, have you anything to report?"

"There . . . there are big monsters in the trees."

Raising an eyebrow, Maura looked questioningly at

the warriors who had brought him.

After exchanging anxious looks, one of the women was brave enough to answer. "The Dinii have arrived, Great Mother, and are resting in the trees near the refugee camp."

Maura beckoned to one of the guards. "Go to the edge of the forest at the back of the refugee camp. Tell the Dinii to assemble at the west side of the city, where we are."

The soldier rushed off to carry out Maura's instructions.

Maura turned her attention back to Akela and instructed an aide-de-camp, "Take this boy to KiKu's wives. Perhaps they can get something else out of him. Tell no one about that boy or KiKu's women."

The Hasan Daeg guards gave the Bhuttanian salute and turned their horses to escort the boy, but not before they heard Maura order, "And tell those women to give this child a bath. He stinks to the heavens."

The soldiers grunted in agreement. Being Hasan Daegians themselves, they could not understand how people could let themselves get so filthy, even if there was a war going on.

It was downright barbaric.

21

Mikkotto loved war.

She loved everything about it—the noise, the confusion, and the smells of sweat, fire, and blood. Even the moans of the dying sounded sweet to her.

And Mikkotto was fearless.

The Bhuttanian soldiers in the city were shocked to realize their brethren serving in Maura's army were determined to support the Blue Queen, even if it meant slaying their relatives.

Mikkotto strode upright on the ramparts, rousing the troops as huge boulders flew past her. "Your kinsmen are bewitched by that she-devil. Fight so that you may kill her and release them from her wicked magic." Her lack of fear encouraged the soldiers to remain at their stations. "Do not shoot. Do not waste your arrows!" she cried out. "Pick up those rocks and cast them back." Anticipating the use of catapults, Mikkotto had ordered her men build their own. Her strategy was to reuse the invaders' boulders against them. Mikkotto had engineers concentrate on destroying the catapults sitting exposed on the plain. After twelve attempts, they were able to damage one of Maura's catapults, thus raising the spirits of the soldiers. Within minutes another one was knocked down and turned on its side.

To further demoralize the Bhuttanians on Maura's side, Mikkotto ordered the soldiers to throw bodies of the dead over the wall with parchments tied to their bodies saying things like—YOU KILLED THIS BHUTTANIAN MOTHER or YOU BUTCHERED THIS INNOCENT CHILD.

Alexanee immediately commanded any Bhuttanian on the front line to report to the Hasan Daegians on the north side of the city, while ordering Anqarians to take their place on the catapults and drag the bodies out of sight and bury them.

He rode to the knoll where Maura had gone back to the platform to observe the assault's progress. He jumped off his horse and asked permission to speak with her privately.

Maura told her advisors to leave, and immediately servants carried steps to the platform and helped them down.

Alexanee leapt up three steps at a time and rushed over to Maura, who remained seated on the aga's throne.

The uultepes, lying on the dais, tensed and growled.

Maura cautioned them to be quiet and bade Alexanee forward.

He walked slowly past the lounging cats and did not flinch as one stuck out his claw and scraped his boots. Alexanee could feel the cat's claws rake across the leather. As the general learned long ago, the uultepes liked to play games and assert their authority over people whenever possible. He ignored them. "Great Mother, I have come to report that the city's walls have yet to be breached. The taking of the city is not at hand."

"I commend your ancestors' ability to build such a remarkable barrier. It is most commendable."

Alexanee bowed. "Unfortunately, we will not be able to take the city today."

Maura stood, snapping her fan shut. "We risk rebellion from our Bhuttanian troops if this continues for long."

"I couldn't agree more. And Mikkotto is catapulting bodies with subversive messages designed to undermine our soldiers' will."

Maura's brow furrowed. "Civilian casualties?"

"Yes, Great Mother."

"Shouldn't all the civilians have been evacuated to the center of the city, away from the fighting?"

"Yes, Great Mother."

"Are we responsible?"

"We cannot tell. Once they splatter on the ground, it is difficult to say what killed them."

"What say ye?"

"I think she is killing women and children, and then throwing them over the wall to make it look like we killed them with our catapults."

"This is very serious. How long before word of this spills out into our main troops?"

"I have reassigned all Bhuttanians who saw the bodies to the Hasan Daegian division on the east side. The rest of the troops are behind our main line. They wouldn't have seen anything."

"Alas, rumors are like water. They flow very quickly in an army. Soldiers are worse than old men sipping colla tea in a café for spreading rumors."

"Yes, Great Mother."

Maura sat back down on her throne thinking. "Water," she murmured. "The river to the north?"

"It supplies the drinking water to the city."

Maura gave the command for all who were watching to face away, and then held a fan to her face so no spy could read her lips. She motioned Alexanee to lean closer. "What if we created a great fire against the wall on the north side, a fire hot enough to heat up the wall? Then we divert the river to rush against the fire."

Alexanee cupped the side of his helmet so no one could read his lips either and completed Maura's thought. "Causing the cold of the water to crack the heated stones."

Maura leaned back on her throne and replied with a whisper of a smile. "Exactly."

"Such a project would take most of the day."

"We don't have hours to spare."

"Can you convince the Dinii to help? With them, we can implement your plan today."

"They are in the forest. I've sent a message for the Dinii to redeploy, but they will probably stay where they are. They prefer the cover of trees, and will do nothing until they have verified that Empress Gitar is living or dead. So they will bide their time. They do not care about our petty war."

Alexanee snarled, "If I start cutting down the trees from the forest to stoke the fire, perhaps they will be motivated to help, since their perches will be taken away. Might they attack us, though?"

"Announce the reason you are felling the trees before cutting. They won't like it, but they won't attack.

Make sure you don't use our stocks of wood. We need ours to make arrows and repair wheels. Is that stand of trees the only wood near Bhuttani?"

"Yes, it was planted so the agas could hunt."

"How will you start the fire?"

"I will use cooking oil and axle grease."

"Make sure our people have adequate protection when building the fire. I don't want our soldiers exposed to arrows from the city when building it."

Alexanee grunted before asking, "One more thing. There are rumors that you assigned two spies to enter the temple of Bhuttu to report on sightings of the Dinii and the Black Cacodemon."

"Did I?"

"I'm sorry you did not trust me enough to let me shoulder this burden with you."

"I wonder how this rumor reached your ears, General. Perhaps you have spies of your own?"

"As you stated, Great Mother, rumors run like water within a military camp."

"Is there anything else you wish to discuss, General Alexanee?"

Realizing this as a dismissal, Alexanee gave the Bhuttanian salute and jumped upon his warhorse from the platform. The horse reared before galloping off with Alexanee firmly on its back.

Maura bit the inside of her cheek as she realized the image of dominance and virility that Alexanee created. Surely many a maiden's heart in the camp fluttered as he rode past on his white stallion. Maura admitted that Alexanee was an arresting man with a keen mind. Besides Mikkotto, he had the potential to become her most dangerous enemy. The sight of Alexanee mastering his stallion turned Maura's thoughts to Dorak.

As Maura's counselors began to ascend the steps to the platform, she waved them away.

Dorak. Dorak. Dorak.

Was he dead?

Was he alive and with Gitar?

What would she do if he were?

Maura knew she could never see Dorak again or her resolve might vanish. Oh, she loved him still. She burned for him—his lips, his arms. She would give anything to hear his melodious voice, to stroke his silky black hair, to have him in her bed, but that could never be. Dorak must never be allowed to ascend to the Bhuttanian throne again.

As soon as Dorak was sighted, Maura had given orders to detain him. A special contingent of Hasan Daegians had been searching for many years.

If captured, Dorak was to be taken to a secret location and tried for war crimes—including the murder of

Queen Abisola and Prince Consort Iasos. Even though he had not given the commands for their deaths, his sheltering of Mikkotto made it possible for their deaths to occur.

At best, Maura could offer Dorak imprisonment at an outlying estate, far away from any large population, and guarded by Hasan Daegian soldiers.

A tear escaped Maura's eye. She dared not wipe it away, lest someone see her.

These were the decisions of queenship that lay heavy upon her shoulders. How could she not make this sacrifice when so many others had done so, including giving their very lives in her service?

Truly, she loved Dorak as no other. Her very flesh called out for his, but she would never touch him again and, Mekonia willing, Maura would never lay eyes upon him either.

Maura was determined to conquer the Bhuttanian people and bend them to her will. After that, she was going to restore order throughout all the empire.

Slowly the rule of law from her courts would supplant the rule of the sword throughout the land, so her citizens might live in peace. But it would never happen with Dorak. Viciousness was bred into him, and moreover, despite Dorak's desire to be a tender ruler, cruelty would win out and consume him, corroding his rule.

Maura thought back to how happy her mother Abisola had been with her father Iasos—a contentment she would never know. She felt dreadfully alone, more alone that she had ever been. Except for her daughter, no one loved her. She knew she would never be loved again, and that was a terrible thing to realize.

Maura straightened her shoulders and thrust out her chin.

What was the matter with her, allowing these maudlin thoughts to overtake her?

She had a war to win.

And she would win it.

22

Dorak followed Zedek.

He was lost in a miasma of a murky and forbidding fog. Putting his hand on the hilt of his dagger gave comfort as Dorak was straining to see the wizard ahead, when out of the corner of his eye he sensed light and movement. He rushed to meet it.

Abruptly, Dorak found himself out of the fog and hovering in the air above a multitude of priests on their knees and chanting. Dorak recognized the chamber. He was in the main hall of the temple of Bhuttu.

On the altar dais, Dorak saw Hilkiah, the high priest of Bhuttu. Hilkiah had officiated at his wedding with Maura and had crowned her as empress. He stood in his official robes, waving his arms and touching something on a gold chain around his neck. Dorak peered harder, trying to discern what Hilkiah was doing, and then inhaled sharply.

The amulet! The very one Dorak had plucked from the body of his father Zoar and used to conjure the Black Cacodemon.

Somehow Hilkiah had gained possession of the amulet!

Dorak realized Hilkiah must be trying to release the wizard from whatever state of suspended animation he had cast.

More important, it seemed to be working!

The air began to shimmer as bands of color formed and buckled. A crescendo of a mournful wail escalated to such a zenith that it culminated in a wave of force which flipped Dorak over and over in the air. He managed to arrest his wild flight by grabbing hold of a column.

Wait! It dawned on Dorak that he had grabbed a physical object. Dorak could feel the cold stone— something solid in his hands.

The incantations were working!

Giddy with the promise of freedom, Dorak watched excitedly as the priests continued their ritual. He could feel his heart pounding so hard against his rib cage, he thought it might it burst from sheer exuberance.

Fierce bolts of lightning shredded the dank temple air below Dorak, but above the heads of the priests.

Heat radiated from the lightning strikes, and the very air in the temple glowed as the fire grew in intensity until brilliant red flames erupted, threatening to engulf the entire chamber. They quickly subsided, and in their wake a shimmering aperture hovered in the air.

Dorak cried out in joy, but his excitement was short-lived.

Out from another column stepped Zedek, murmuring an invocation. As he made his way to the portal, the wizard morphed into a fearsome creature, complete with scales, claws, and fangs.

A dragon!

Realizing Zedek was making his way to escape, Dorak pushed away from the column, rushing toward the monster.

Just as Zedek was stepping through, Dorak grabbed his scaly neck and pulled the wizard back.

Dorak could not allow Zedek to pass into the dimension of the living.

Even if Dorak had to sacrifice his own life!

23

KiKu was asleep.

He had dozed off, slumped against a wall. Hearing the loud peal of a gong, he shook himself awake and quickly took in his surroundings. Had he given himself away?

Realizing he was still hidden and safe, KiKu indulged himself by giving way to emotion. He would have snapped the necks of any of his operatives if they had fallen asleep on a critical mission. Now he had done the same. Shame welled up within him.

KiKu thought back to his wives. They were facing acute danger, and he had almost added to their peril. He thought of Maura, struggling to rescue a world. He might have easily failed them all.

He had to admit he was getting old, and intrigue no longer thrilled him. The notorious spylord would rather be in his tent, sitting by a nice fire, and surrounded by the chatter of his wives.

The hetmaan wanted the war to be over, and the slaughter to stop. KiKu was sick of death and senseless suffering.

When the war was over, KiKu would take his wives to live in Hasan Daeg. He knew Maura would reward him with sanctuary, even a large estate with a grand house—perhaps Mikkotto's estate. KiKu grinned at the irony of that. Yes, he would ask for Mikkotto Sumsumitoyo's land and palace. KiKu knew Maura would delight in that.

The spylord had to put those thoughts aside, because the chanting of the priests was growing in volume and intensity. KiKu peeked from his hiding place.

The very air above the priests was transforming. It began to sparkle and vibrate, supplanted by what looked like a thick liquid one could almost touch.

Astonished, KiKu shot a look at Hilkiah, who was standing on the altar, carefully cradling the amulet and muttering with his eyes closed. All the other priests were kneeling on the floor, ardently chanting incantations with their eyes closed as well.

It was apparent Hilkiah had learned how to manipulate the amulet, and it was working. The hole in the fabric of the temple's dank air was expanding.

KiKu put his hand on his dagger, ready to strike.

The entire temple shuddered violently.

The priests' eyes flew open, and they gaped up in amazement.

An enormous reptilian leg shot forth from the roiling darkness above the priests. Then a second leg punched through the portal, followed by a spiked tail uncoiling and whipping dangerously.

Some of the priests moaned while others screamed joyfully and danced upon their mats.

Bhuttu would be so pleased.

They had called forth a dragon!

24

Timon stumbled.

He used a massive column to steady himself before lurching into the ceremonial chamber, but no one noticed because their attention was riveted on the hole emerging in the smoke-filled air of the temple.

Timon followed their gaze and gasped.

The space above them flashed while pulsating bands of color fluctuated halfway between the ceiling and the floor until a loud noise thundered, sounding like a cracked whip.

The portal was opening!

A hole, devoid of color, undulated and grew larger and larger, until a monstrous leg and tail emerged.

Before Timon could react, KiKu sprang from his hiding place and threw himself at Hilkiah. Timon expected KiKu to be repelled by the protective aura

Hilkiah created about his person, but the High Priest, weakened by hours of continuous chanting and ritual, could not sustain the shield as before.

KiKu tussled with Hilkiah, trying to snatch the amulet off his neck, but the High Priest was still stronger. The spylord struggled to subdue Hilkiah, who screamed for help. In the melee, KiKu dropped his dagger.

Several of Hilkiah's attendants sprang to his aid, only to be beaten back by Timon, who rushed behind the High Priest.

A blast of frigid air knocked everyone down as the Dinii, long captives of the netherworld, exploded through the portal with such force that many hit the back wall of the chamber and were knocked unconscious, plummeting to the stone floor. The Dinii, who managed to avoid flying into walls, descended and formed a tight circle around their fallen comrades. Others hovered in confusion looking for a way out.

The priests advanced upon the Dinii.

The powerful Dinii fended off the priests, picking them up and breaking their necks, but the priests, fueled by religious frenzy, threw themselves at KiKu, Timon, and the Dinii.

Losing his grasp on Hilkiah, KiKu made a final move to break Hilkiah's leg. A sickening snap sounded in the din as the High Priest's thighbone cracked, causing the High Priest to howl in pain. More priests ran onto the altar, mauling KiKu and Timon.

A fierce blow to the head knocked Timon down, leaving him defenseless. Three priests leapt on him and bludgeoned him in the kidneys. Overcome by the intense pain, Timon feared he might lose consciousness until he spied KiKu's dagger. Lunging for it, he barely caught it by its blade and pulled it to him. Ignoring the searing pain as the blade sliced his hand, Timon swept his arm upward, slashing the throat of one of the priests holding him down. The other two priests stepped back in alarm, freeing Timon to careen toward Hilkiah, sending the knife blade deep into the priest's back.

Seeing his opportunity, KiKu snatched the amulet off Hilkiah's neck.

Another freezing blast burst forth from the portal, which was pulsating wildly as Empress Gitar and Prince Iegani swept out to join their comrades.

Gitar, having watched events from the other side of the portal before flying through, shouted orders for her warriors to save KiKu and Timon.

The Dinii, led by Yeti, plowed through the priests by bashing their heads against the mighty stone columns holding up the roof. As the Dinii, KiKu, and Timon fought for their lives, the portal groaned and quaked.

The empress moved to reenter the portal to seek

Dorak, when Iegani pulled her back. "Gitar, think of your people. Dorak means nothing to us."

Resigned to let Dorak meet his fate, Gitar pushed her uncle away and flapped her powerful wings to hover in the air while giving orders to the Dinii.

A great crash sounded, and the walls trembled as if in an earthquake. Gitar was hurled against a wall, breaking one of her wings, slamming her to the temple floor.

Enraged that their High Priest had been slain, the infuriated priests set upon the wounded Dinii empress, but they were no match for Gitar. Even though weakened, she seized her attackers with her talons and tore their heads off.

Iegani, with several other Dinii, forced their way through the mob surrounding her. Even though there were close to a thousand priests, novices, and attendants, they were no match for the Dinii, who caused the blood of the slain to coat the floor. The Dinii made quick work of them, throwing their dead bodies into a pile in the middle of the floor until they formed a barricade which the surviving priests had to climb over in order to reach the fray.

All the while the temple quivered and moaned as walls crumbled and tall columns toppled over.

Gitar scanned the chamber for an exit. With the help

of Iegani and Toppo, Gitar followed other Dinii fleeing the temple. Yeti and Tarsus were the last Dinii to fly out of the temple, carrying Timon and KiKu, who was clutching the severed head of Hilkiah.

They did not see the portal quake one last time and disgorge a battling Zedek and Dorak, locked in fierce combat.

Zedek, now in human form, pulled away from Dorak. "Fool! Don't you see the temple is destroying itself?"

Dorak cried back, "I don't care. You must not be allowed to live!"

Zedek held his arm out straight with his palm flat, pointing toward Dorak, unleashing a white-hot bolt of energy, which slammed Dorak against a falling column, knocking him senseless. Zedek recited an incantation and disappeared.

Dorak, coming to his senses, lurched to his feet to resume the fight, but realized Zedek was gone. Climbing over dead bodies and rubble, Dorak made his way through the maze of debris until he came out onto the city street as the lofty ceiling of the temple twisted and collapsed.

The ground shook, and the grand temple of Bhuttu inclined to one side, seemingly frozen for a moment before collapsing in a ground-shaking rumble of dust and debris.

The aga bowed his head and whispered a Bhuttanian prayer for the dead. He wondered if all the Dinii made it out, but was sure he had glimpsed them fleeing the main chamber when he fell out of the portal.

Hearing the whoosh of arrows piercing the air and the crash of boulders pounding against the walls of the city, Dorak knew Maura must be attacking. He quickly weighed his options. If he tried to contact Maura, Dorak knew he would surely be killed by his enemies in the Hasan Daegian court before he could reach her.

No, it would be better if he could make his way to the Imperial Palace. Dorak hesitated. If he occupied the throne, the fighting might stop. But what if Maura had given orders for him to be killed on sight? Dorak realized the Dinii from the temple would immediately find Maura and inform her that he was alive. She need only to give the order, and every Dinii would hunt him down.

If he were in Maura's place, that's was what he would do. Dorak's heart sank. He knew Maura loved him, but he had placed her in a terrible position. He'd left her with no choice but to kill him or take him prisoner.

Dorak took a deep breath. The only thing he could do now was save his son and flee. Perhaps once Maura took control of the city he could contact her and work out some sort of a treaty. He had no doubt Jezra and their son were in the palace. She would have had to stay to keep the city's soldiers loyal and willing to fight Maura.

A man running in the street stopped in his tracks staring at Dorak. "My lord, are you . . ."

Dorak extended his hand as if offering a greeting, but as the man came within reach, he grabbed the man's tunic and broke his neck, saying softly, "No, I'm not, my friend." He gently lowered the man's body before rushing to the palace.

He had to save his son. Dorak pleaded to any god that would listen, "Let me do one honorable thing before I die. Let me save my son."

But the gods were not listening.

25

Maura heard shouting.

The cries were coming from soldiers pointing at the sky.

Maura bolted from her throne as counselors and foreign dignitaries moved to get a better look. They all looked toward the heavens, watching as a black cloud shot up from the city into the sky with a great cacophony reverberating throughout the land. Even those working the catapults stopped and gaped.

"The Dinii!" shouted the Hasan Daegians, pointing and waving their arms. The rest of the army cheered while the Bhuttanians winced and looked away. They hadn't forgotten the terror they felt when Maura and the Dinii first attacked them at the wall of mist on the border of Hasan Daeg.

"They're on our side now, chum," remarked a Bhuttanian private, nudging his companion, who looked upon the ascending swarm with dread.

"Let's hope they don't have a change of heart and rip our heads off," his friend replied.

Another great cry came from within Bhuttani, probably since the city's residents had never seen a Dini. The city's defense forces began shooting at them immediately.

Alexanee shouted at his men working the catapults to get back to work, hoping to provide covering fire for the Dinii leaving the city.

The cloud flew straight up as Maura knew they would. If confused or in danger, the Dinii always flew straight up. To the right of the city another massive cloud ascended.

Maura knew it was Chaun Maaun and the rest of the Dinii rushing to meet Gitar. They would fly beyond the clouds and hover until a decision was made. Maura hoped they would return to the camp Maura had set up for them and not fly away to the Forbidden Zone, leaving the war and its terrors behind.

Maura called for her palanquin. She urgently desired to run to the Dinii's camp, but knew she had to ceremonially welcome Gitar, who, as the Dinii empress, had higher status. All things had to be done according to protocol, since many eyes watched, eager to find fault. To reassure her forces, she must project serene confidence when entering the Dinii camp.

Alexanee watched while eight Hasan Daegian female soldiers, all equal in height, bore the royal palanquin on their broad shoulders. Although he knew the Dinii were a military necessity, he despised them, and hoped they would fly back to the mountains, once the war was over. Alexanee hated their high-pitched voices and the dreadful clicking noise they made when talking to one another. He was repulsed that they had feathers where there should have been flesh, and feared their retractable claws that could rip a man to shreds.

Let the Hasan Daegians make all the treaties they wanted with those loathsome creatures. He wanted no part of the Dinii. As soon as possible, Alexanee would use his considerable influence over Maura to have them excluded from Bhuttan, because he never wanted to see another Dini as long as he lived.

If Maura would not see fit to send the Dinii away, perhaps he would circulate a rumor his spies had uncovered to undermine her. He rubbed his chin, thinking.

But would anyone believe that Maura and Chaun Maaun had once been lovers? The very idea was ludicrous. He didn't think the rumor had merit, but if one repeated a lie often enough, people believed it, and it would put the reign of Princess Dyanna at risk. After all, who was her real father?

And if one pounded a wall long enough, it would fall. "Put your backs into it, men!" yelled Alexanee as he peered through a field glass.

Was that a tiny crack in the wall? No, he concluded. Alexanee slapped his saddle horn in frustration. Right now he wanted Maura to convince the Dinii to help with the river. He needed their assistance, or the taking of Bhuttani would be delayed.

Alexanee would work with the Black Cacodemon himself if that's what it took to take Bhuttani and install Maura as the aganess.

Then, when the time was right, Alexanee would make his move, but for now he had to bide his time. He spat on the ground at the thought of a foreigner on the ancient throne of the Bhuttanian agas.

And a female foreigner at that!

26

Maura reached the Dinii camp.

By the time she exited her palanquin, all the Dinii had retreated from the sky to the shelter of the tents Maura had provided behind the protection of her vast army.

Servants were serving platters of raw meat and flagons of ale to ravenous Dinii while the wounded were attended by the women from the House of Magi who applied healing salves and bound wounds.

Maura concluded from the number of wounded Dinii that a fierce battle had been fought in the temple. Walking through the camp, she heard her name whispered as the Dinii recognized her. "Maura. Great Mother. It's Maura. Little sparrow."

Whispers turned to shouts as the Dinii stood up from their stools or jumped off perches. Several tried to embrace Maura, but were held back by her guards. Reaching the royal tent, Maura formally requested an audience with Gitar. Standing before Gitar's private quarters, she waited patiently, thinking a private audience could be rejected. After all, Gitar might hold her responsible for her people's suffering.

A Dini sentry opened the flap of the tent and bade Maura to enter.

Empress Gitar sat, being tended by a healer who was setting her broken wing.

Realizing that Gitar was injured, Maura cried out, "Mother!" and ran to her, collapsing at her feet in a heap.

"My little sparrow," cooed Gitar, stroking Maura's windblown hair. "My little sparrow. It has been so long. So long. Let me look at you."

"Get up, child," Maura recognized the unmistakable voice in her mind. Rising and looking about, Maura whispered, "Iegani?" Seeing him standing in a corner and smiling warmly at her, Maura ran and wrapped him in a hug.

Iegani patted Maura's head with great affection. "Is this anyway for a great warrior to act? Haven't we taught you better?"

Wiping away her tears, Maura pulled away, nodding. "I have looked for you so long, and now to see you again . . . alive. This is a great blessing from Mekonia."

"That hurts," Gitar snapped at the healer, giving the woman a quick peck on the hand.

The healer drew back in astonishment.

Maura exclaimed, "Second mother of my heart! Let me minister to you as only I can."

Gitar gently pushed Maura away. "No! You must conserve all your strength for this war. That is most important. You must not waste your energy. I am in capable hands."

Maura cautioned the healer. "Empress Gitar and the royal court of the Dinii are to be your only patients. You must see to Empress Gitar's every need."

The healer bowed, "Yes, Great Mother."

Gitar scoffed, "It is nothing, little sparrow."

Maura looked questioningly at the healer.

"The empress has sustained a minor break in the wing. She should be whole in a couple of weeks," replied the healer, all the while staring at the floor and trying not to tremble with fear.

Maura asked, "You cannot fly?"

"With help, I can."

"We shall make your stay as comfortable as possible." Maura turned to the healer. "Leave us now. And I warn you not to breathe a word of what you see or hear in this tent. As far as anyone is concerned, Empress

Gitar is resting, and that is all that will be said."

"Yes, Great Mother. I understand and will obey."

"Leave us now."

Once the healer removed herself from the tent, Maura picked up a stool from a corner and sat before Gitar. "You must have many questions as I do." She grasped Gitar's hand and held it to her cheek. "I thought I had killed that beast, but Zedek must have uttered a spell with his last breath. When I turned, you were no longer there."

"I understand it has been years, but seemed only hours to those of us bound in the netherworld."

Maura nodded. "Yes, second mother of my heart. I have been searching for three years."

"You are now ruler of all of Kaseri?"

"Except for Bhuttani."

Iegani intercepted, "This is the final battle of the civil war?"

Maura turned toward him. "Yes. Once I capture Bhuttani and imprisoned Jezra and her son, this nightmare will be over."

"It is what we hoped for, little sparrow," chirped Gitar. "All that I and your mother, Queen Abisola, had sought for so many years. Our efforts have now borne fruit." She looked at Iegani. "We can go home to the mountains and begin anew."

Iegani reminded, "My dear niece, you are forgetting our companion in the netherworld?"

"I have not forgotten. We were not alone. Dorak was with us."

Maura gasped, "Dorak!"

"Yes, little sparrow. He helped us in many ways."

"Where is he now?"

Gitar shook her head. "I know not, my child. The priests opened the portal through which we escaped. When I saw Dorak last, he was battling a dragon which I suspect was Zedek. I don't know if he made it through or not."

"If he didn't," said Maura, "Dorak may well be lost forever. The temple of Bhuttu has collapsed. It is a pile of rubble."

"That would solve one of your thorniest problems," commented Iegani.

"Iegani! Dorak was Maura's husband," sputtered Gitar, shocked at his bluntness.

"Yes, and he was the cause of the loss of our home and the death of your daughters."

"And the loss of my eye."

Maura looked up in surprise. "Chaun Maaun, I didn't realize you were present." She quickly stood with her hand on her dagger.

Empress Gitar growled, "Stop it, both of you. If

Maura hadn't married Dorak, she never would have been in a position to become empress. We all did what we had to do."

"I must take my leave and let you rest, Empress," said Maura, ignoring Chaun Maaun, who loomed menacingly over her. "Before I do, I wish to present you these tokens of my esteem and gratitude." Maura called for her servants, who quickly entered the tent and carefully placed several boxes before her.

Maura opened one of them. "Diamond dust for your personal adornment."

Gitar clicked happily in the Dinii language at the sight of the glittering powder.

Pleased to see Gitar excited over the crushed diamonds, Maura opened another box and withdrew a stunning tiara with a myriad of colored stones. "A crown fit for an empress."

"Ooh," replied Gitar, reaching for it and placing it on her head.

"I will take my leave now," announced Maura. "But before I go, my forces need your help to take the city. We cannot get past the gate."

"We have sacrificed enough," snarled Chaun Maaun, with a downward twist of his mouth. "As soon as my mother is able, we shall fly to the Forbidden Zone."

Gitar threw up her hand to silence her impetuous

son. She was weary of his continuous harping over his wounded pride. "The Forbidden Zone will not protect us if Maura is not the ruler of Bhuttan. We must see this through to the bitter end."

She turned to Maura. "I pledged that I would do everything in my power to make the Lahorians' prophecy come true. They said you would become a great warrior and rule the world. I will complete my promise to them and to your mother. Command the Dinii as you see fit. My people are yours."

Maura bowed deeply to Gitar. Before leaving the tent, she assumed an impassive countenance, once more showing no emotion, even though her heart sang twin songs of joy and trepidation at the same time.

Dorak was alive!

Dorak was alive!

27

Chaun Maaun protested.

"Mother! Let us leave this land of doom."

"My son," Gitar replied despairingly. "You always pluck the same string on your lute. It's time to play a different tune."

"This war has cost us our home and the lives of my sisters!"

"This war has cost Maura the lives of her parents, Abisola and Iasos."

"That's nothing compared to our sorrow."

"You are thinking only of yourself, Chaun Maaun. I was told by the Lahorians many years ago that our world was open to destruction by a force from the east. I have dedicated most of my life to making the sacrifices needed to stop the Bhuttanians.

"Maura is key to our survival. I know you once

loved Maura, and now feel bitter hatred for her because you believe she abandoned you, but I tell you this . . . your marriage to her was never to be. Your destiny follows a different path. You must marry your own kind. Maura was right to marry Dorak."

"You knew about us?"

"Chaun Maaun, everyone knew about the two of you."

Chaun Maaun looked stricken.

"After the war is won, I intend to sign a new treaty with Maura, recognizing her as rightful sovereign. I also will be relinquishing our guardianship over the Hasan Daegians. They no longer need us to watch over them. We must be concerned with rebuilding our territory in the mountains and reinvigorating our people. Our numbers are too few now. Our people must conceive and bring up new generations."

Iegani added, "Yes, we must revitalize our culture, and you must not do anything to jeopardize our future, Chaun Maaun. Maura must be convinced to sign this new treaty."

"Does she know of your intentions, Mother?"

"No, but that's why we must stay and render assistance. We will need the help of the Hasan Daegians to recover from the devastation of this war. Once we have accomplished this feat and our people are strong again, we will retreat to our city in the Forbidden Zone forever, and hopefully never see another non-Dini being again unless we desire it."

Chaun Maaun asked, "Will we rebuild City of the Peaks?"

Gitar cast a glance at Iegani. "I think it best we go back to the Forbidden Zone and rebuild Atetelco. I don't think the Lahorians will bother us again, since we have come to Maura's aid. That was their charge to us, and we have complied."

Gitar stood and put her arms around her son. "Enough of this morbid talk. I tell you this, my son. Cherish the time you spent with Maura. Don't ever forget it. It will warm your nights when you are old, but put it behind you for now. Please, son. For all our sakes, move beyond your grief."

Gitar pulled Chaun Maaun closer to her. "Believe me when I say you will be happy again. Not every day will be dark and full of woe. Things change, as does one's heart."

"I have shamed you, Mother."

"I never felt shame." Gitar smiled at Chaun Maaun. "I have felt concern, but you must follow my guidance now. Maura has no one in this world. Everyone she has ever loved is gone, except for her child. She needs our help. She must emerge victorious from this war. Help her, Chaun Maaun. Help the woman you once loved."

"I love her still, but Mother, I must confess I hate her as well. Sometimes I think my hate for her is stronger than my love ever was." Chaun Maaun glanced at his mother's horrified face. He bent down and kissed her hand. "But for you, I will do as you ask."

Iegani stepped forward. "At present, Maura needs help to divert a river."

Chaun Maaun asked, "Why don't we overtake the city by night and kill the soldiers?"

"Because it would cause mutiny within Maura's army. The Bhuttanians on her side would rebel if they saw us perpetrate such a slaughter. The taking of the city must be done with as little bloodshed as possible," replied Gitar.

Chaun Maaun replied dully, "That is unfortunate. We could make the city ours in a matter of hours."

"Yes, 'tis true, but there are other things to consider," replied Iegani. "Take command of those Dinii who are fresh and help the soldiers in the forest. The rest of us will join you once we have rested and eaten."

Chaun Maaun bowed. "I will obey. You have only to command."

28

Dorak ran through the streets.

A small gang of soldiers chased him, obviously planning to beat and rob him, but Dorak outran them, finally hiding in a butcher's shop that had already been looted.

Peering between broken shutters and watching the men search for him, Dorak stifled laughter, realizing the absurdity of his situation. The Aga of Bhuttan was in a butcher's shop hiding from his soldiers. "Oh, Maura, if you could see me now."

After the soldiers gave up and left, Dorak waited a few minutes and then ventured out into the street. He didn't meet anyone beyond a few women darting from their homes to fill their water jars from the few fountains still running. He thought it humane that Maura had not cut off the water supply yet, but he knew that would change if the city did not surrender soon.

The relentless pounding of stones hurled against the west wall strained Dorak's nerves, and he put his hands over his ears. As he traveled deeper into the center of the city, the sound of the catapults diminished, but still reverberated off the buildings' walls. Dorak lengthened his stride. He had to reach Jezra before Maura did.

Once he was within sight of the palace, Dorak climbed onto the roof of the abandoned home of one of his generals. Crawling to the edge of the roof, he saw scattered squads guarding the palace entrances.

Scrutinizing the men's demeanor, Dorak decided they were too unruly and skittish for him to approach. He thought them capable of running a sword through him for the fun of it before he could identify himself. Dorak decided it was best to bide his time until he could approach the palace under cover of darkness. He'd use his great-grandfather's secret tunnel located on the next street.

In the meantime, he went back downstairs to search for a suitable place to hide until nighttime. Finding a larder full of food, he stuffed himself while drinking the general's colla tea and then wine. Finally satiated, Dorak fell asleep exhausted, even amidst the pounding of the west wall and gate, which he was certain would hold. Known to him, but unbeknownst to Maura and even any of the Bhuttanian generals, all gates and walls were bound by magic. No boulder, no matter how large and powerful, would breach the walls of Bhuttani.

Unless a miracle occurred for Maura, the walls would stand.

29

Jezra shrieked.

"Can't you make them stop?" she cried out. "I can't stand that constant pounding."

Zedek replied, "Yes, I can, but I think it's better if I conserve my powers. You can hardly hear the noise, and I think we should let Maura's army use up their arsenal and exhaust themselves. It does very little harm to let them continue."

Jezra threw herself into a chair, pouting. "Where have you been all this time? I could have used your help."

"I am sorry, Jezra. I was inescapably detained." Zedek studied Jezra closely. Something was not right with her. Her eyes appeared vacant, and her entire demeanor seemed strained. It had to be more than the little pounding at the west gate that set her teeth on edge. He wondered if she was drugged . . . or simply losing her mind.

"You will address me by the title aganess."

Zedek bowed. "Forgive me, Aganess."

Jezra nodded. "What do you intend to do about Maura?"

The wizard stifled an urge to yawn. Dealing with people with such limited insight drained him. "At the moment . . . nothing."

"What? Nothing!"

"Calm yourself, my sweet girl. Your general, Mikkotto, seems to have everything under control."

Jezra snarled, "I told you not to be familiar with me."

Zedek took a deep breath to restore his tranquility and bowed slightly. "Forgive me, my lady. My brain is addled after being away for such a long period. May I excuse myself? I must eat and rest."

"But what about the assaults on the walls? Sooner or later they will fall."

"No, Aganess, they won't."

"What do you mean?"

Zedek laughed. "Trust me. The walls will hold . . . and hold . . . and hold," he said, gliding out of the room, leaving Jezra glaring after him.

30

Alexanee was relieved.

The Dinii were no longer in the forest. The last thing Alexanee wanted was to coax huge birdmen with razor-sharp talons from their perches. "Throw your backs into it, men!" he shouted from his majestic warhorse.

He felt even more relieved when his lieutenant related that all the Dinii had gathered in a camp the Great Mother established for them in the rear lines. However, the cutting down of the ancient trees and transporting them to the north wall of Bhuttani was more laborious than he had anticipated.

Pulling off his helmet, he wiped the sweat from his brow. Regardless of how many men they threw at this task, the fire at the wall was not going to happen today. It was too monumental a task.

Alexanee knew his men. Sooner or later the Bhuttanians under his command would rebel. It was only a
matter of time before they turned on him and Maura.
Only a matter of time.

He turned in his saddle, studying the city. Why were
the walls of Bhuttani not falling? It was almost unimagi-
nable that they still stood.

The general sighed and gratefully accepted water
from a water boy, careful not to touch the nozzle of the
leather bag with his lips while squeezing it to squirt
water into his mouth. That was one thing he had
learned from the fanatically clean Hasan Daegians, who
insisted the communal water dippers and buckets be
abolished. He did notice that his men were ill less
frequently since they adopted this new custom.

Alexanee also squirted water on his neck and face
before handing the bag back to the boy. Why was he
thinking such nonsense at a time like this? He didn't
understand his own thoughts sometimes.

After watching thirty men descend upon a fallen
tree, using axes to section it into manageable pieces
before throwing them into a wagon, Alexanee turned
his attention to the sun. It was after midday. His
stomach lurched.

They would never get the fire at the north wall started before dark, and even that might be unattainable.

Hearing a loud whoosh, the general cupped a hand over his eyes, looking up into the sky. The hot air stirred, and the plumes on his helmet fluttered while his horse whinnied and pawed the ground nervously.

His men shouted and hurriedly back away from the logs they had been working on as thousands of Dinii descended upon the ground and into the tops of standing trees. Immediately, the Dinii picked up the heavy logs with their taloned feet and flew off with them.

Feeling another sudden breeze, Alexanee cast his eyes upward to see Chaun Maaun hovering just above his horse, causing the alarmed beast to rear up. It was all Alexanee could do to keep the horse from bolting while keeping his seat.

He was sure Chaun Maaun meant to unsettle the beast. "Gods," he muttered darkly, looking at the fearsome creature, whose face was marred by one wrecked eye. It took all his will not to shudder at Chaun Maaun's fearsome appearance.

Relishing the shock on Alexanee's face, all Chuan Maaun muttered before flying off was, "We will help."

And help they did.

The Dinii searched for fallen and decayed trees, which would burn better than the green wood the Bhuttanians were cutting. Soon the sky was littered with black dots of flying Dinii carrying colossal logs with as little effort as children carrying a feather.

Alexanee watched while Dinii threw the logs against the north wall and returned for more. Even though the city's men were shooting arrows, the Dinii were too quick, and soon the Bhuttanians fled the parapets when a couple of huge logs were hurled at their heads.

Alexanee chuckled. He had to admit his warriors still might have a chance to end this civil war today, and he hated the thought he had been aided by these birdmen, but Zoar had drilled into him—the enemy of my enemy is my friend. Though it might stick in his craw, the Dinii might be the key to victory.

31

A courier ran with a scroll.

She found Maura departing from the Dinii camp far behind the main army. Kneeling, she raised her arm to hand the scroll to the empress riding in the veiled palanquin.

One of Maura's guards grabbed the scroll, waving the courier away.

"What is it?" asked Maura from inside the palanquin.

"Great Mother, a message."

Maura stuck her hand through the curtains, grabbing the scroll. Expecting a message from Alexanee, Maura drew back in surprise when she saw the seal. The message was from Meagan of Skujpor.

Come quick. The Dinii dropped off two bolts of cloth to your tent and they are torn beyond belief.

Shaking her head at Meagan's lame attempt to hide the message's intent, Maura ordered a horse to ride back to her tent. It would be faster and more expedient.

Her first lieutenant hopped off her pony and surrendered it to Maura, doubling with another rider.

Maura jumped on the little pony and gave the command to gallop. She must reach her tent with all haste.

What awaited her, she did not know, but knew Meagan would not have sent the missive if not of dire importance.

Had her warriors located Dorak?

Was he waiting for her?

Had something happened to Dyanna, her baby?

What did it mean *torn beyond belief*?

As she galloped, her guards rode behind holding aloft the Imperial banners while the uultepes loped beside her pony, excited by Maura's agitated demeanor.

Warriors of all nationalities stood and waved streamers, scarves, and flags as Maura galloped past, hoping she was riding fast because the battle was to begin soon. They were restless with boredom, and the strain of waiting was beginning to wear on them.

Maura brandished her sword in the air as a gesture of encouragement, realizing her troops' morale might be on the wane. Hoping the news waiting at her tent was good news, Maura quickened the pace.

Still, Maura's heart was filled with dread.

She feared whatever waiting for her was not good.

32

Maura jumped off the pony.

Striding into her private chambers, Maura slapped her riding quirt against her knee-high boots.

"Where is Meagan of Skujpor?" she demanded to know.

Several of Maura's young male servants whispered in unison while pointing, "In your chambers."

Why would Meagan take anyone into Maura's private bedchamber unless it was someone or something she was trying to hide? The only people allowed into the inner chamber were Maura's servants, who were very trustworthy.

"My bedroom?" questioned Maura. "Oh Mekonia, it must be my child who in danger!"

Maura ran through the various compartments that made up her tent, throwing open curtains until she came to her private chamber.

Almost all the lamps in her bedroom had been dampened, with Meagan leaning over the bed administering a draft to someone in Maura's bed.

"Is it the princess? Is she ill?"

Meagan looked up from her ministrations and pointed to a dark corner of the chamber.

Maura whirled around.

KiKu, attended by one of her male servants, was sitting at a table calmly eating a roasted boaep.

KiKu nodded, but did not rise or kowtow.

Maura ordered, "Get out, everyone!"

All the servants scurried away except for Meagan.

"You, get out too," barked Maura.

"Great Mother, I can't leave my patient. It is essential that I stay," challenged Meagan.

Maura huffed with frustration.

Didn't Meagan and KiKu know that being familiar and neglecting protocol affected her prestige with the troops and the people? Still, Maura had to push those thoughts away as she hurried to the bed.

Was Meagan treating Dorak?

Would she have to make a terrible decision regarding her husband so soon?

Meagan stood aside as Maura peered down.

"Timon!" Maura gasped, shocked at his wrecked

condition. "My poor lad." She turned to Meagan. "What is wrong with him?"

"His heartbeat is faint," saucily replied Meagan of Skujpor, "but he is in surprisingly good condition for someone who's supposed to be dead." She pointed at KiKu drinking ale and wiping his mouth with the tablecloth. "And didn't he and his wives leave in a huff many months ago?"

"I don't know what you're babbling about, healer. Timon Ben Ibin Moab is dead. He died from a borax attack in the mountains, and Prince KiKu from Hittal *was* sent away from court for his unruliness."

"Yet, here lies Royal Scribe Timon, and there sits Prince KiKu." Meagan gave her queen a sharp look. "But I can see where I've made my mistake with these two vagabonds. Just to be on the safe side, you'd better tell your servants not to mention seeing them, or it will be all over the camp within an hour."

"I need not worry there. My servants are bound to secrecy. Besides the uultepes are with them."

"I hope those cats are not using those poor boys as scratching posts." Meagan pushed Maura out of the way to attend Timon who was moaning.

Maura strode over to KiKu. "Good to see you alive, my fine friend. I knew you would not fail me."

KiKu ignored Maura and kept eating.

"Will you not speak to me, friend? Surely, you paid no heed to my chatter with Meagan? I am relieved to see both you and Timon."

KiKu pushed his plate away and picked up a wet clay tablet with a stylus.

"Writing on a tablet? Must we resort to that old spy trick? I can read your mind if you push hard enough," said Maura, irritated at the subterfuge. She needed information immediately.

KiKu shook his head.

"All right then. Have it your way," sighed Maura. "I have seen Empress Gitar and the rest of the freed Dinii."

KiKu shook his head nervously.

Maura was so frustrated that she almost shook her oldest and most trusted counselor. "Hetmaan, I don't have time for this. If information you have, then give it to me freely. I must make haste."

With a shaky hand, KiKu began to write.

Maura glowered at KiKu as he wrote. He had lost a great deal of weight. The little potbelly KiKu had acquired was gone. There were deep creases around his forehead and mouth, and when he looked at her, his dark eyes seemed haunted. KiKu looked old and used up. He must have suffered a great deal to free the Dinii.

Maura instantly regretted her sharp words, but her

face remained immobile. Many people had to sacrifice for her and Princess Dyanna, but she showed no regret to KiKu. Regret was a luxury Maura could not afford, but she was not without compassion.

"Oh, KiKu. My brave KiKu," she whispered, putting her hand on his shaking arm.

A tear slipped from KiKu's eye. His hands trembled so, KiKu feared he would not be able to communicate by the written code he had taught Maura, but once he had delivered the information to Maura, he was done. He shot a look at Maura, who smiled warmly at him. Immediately, KiKu felt better.

Pointing at Maura's face, he claimed, "That's the smile of a young girl. I've seen that smile before. It is as though the sun broke through the clouds. I thought I would never see that girl again. I'm glad to see she still exists."

"You are safe now," Maura reassured him.

KiKu whispered, "No, we're not, Maura. The Black Cacodemon was trapped with the Dinii. He lives."

"So, it is true that demon still exists. If only I had been a few seconds earlier with the deathblow, I might have saved us all much suffering. Tell me more."

KiKu hesitated.

Maura coaxed, "Do not fear to tell me what is already known. The enemy has the same information.

Speak freely to me."

"It was neither Timon nor I who freed the Dinii. Zedek somehow manipulated the priests into freeing us."

"The amulet was of no help?" asked Maura, astounded.

"Yes, it was, but only at the very end of the priests' incantations. I believe the amulet focused the energy of the incantations to open a portal into another world."

"Why did Empress Gitar not tell me of this?"

"For the same reason, I hesitate to speak out loud now. Ask no more questions. We may be watched and overheard, even here. Magic," warned KiKu before returning to his clay tablet describing the priests opening the portal allowing the Dinii burst through and fight their way out of the temple.

Maura was bursting with a myriad of questions, but fought to remain patient. If KiKu thought they might be overheard by magic, that meant he believed the evil wizard Zedek had escaped and was at large somewhere in the city, but her time with KiKu was limited. She had to get back to the front or questions would be asked.

"Tell me what you witnessed."

KiKu began writing of the last moments in the temple before its collapse.

Maura grabbed KiKu's hand. "This is foolish, my

friend. The hardship had addled your brain. We need not fear discussing the past. I can understand caution discussing battle plans and our next move, but the past cannot be undone. Speak to me." Maura threw caution to the wind. "Get to the important stuff, man. Was Dorak with the Dinii?"

KiKu shrugged and spoke only in clipped sentences. "Did not see Dorak. Can't confirm."

"Did the Dinii speak of him?"

"They said nothing, but carried us out of the temple, dropping us off here."

"Empress Gitar said she saw Dorak fighting with a dragon before she flew through the portal."

"I did not see this. I am sorry to report the temple collapsed. Dorak might not have made it out in time."

Maura closed her eyes and felt grateful. Dorak crushed by the rubble of the fallen temple would solve a terrible dilemma. She would not have to make the awful decision to execute him. Yet, Maura felt her heart tighten at the thought of Dorak's death and turned away from KiKu, hiding her emotions.

"Where is the amulet now?" asked Maura, wanting to change the subject.

"Here." KiKu leaned over and picked up the lid of a platter.

Maura's eyes widened.

On the platter lay the head of Hilkiah with the amulet placed upon his forehead.

"A gift for you, Great Mother."

"For the love of the goddess Mekonia! You know I don't relish such gifts."

"You don't want my gifts? I went to a lot of trouble retrieving them."

"You know what I'm talking about."

"Don't scold me, Maura. We are both capable of great mischief, and have engaged in much to get you thus far. If you don't appreciate my gifts, I will take my trophy with me, but there is no need to reproach me . . . or I shall reproach you," huffed KiKu, insulted.

"Great Mother!" called Meagan of Skujpor.

Maura jumped up and ran over to the bed. She peered down at Timon's feverish body. He was covered with nasty cuts and painful-looking bruises. Blood was seeping from wounds on his head. Maura gingerly touched his forehead with her fingers. "He looks gravely ill."

"The boy is slipping away," Meagan said. "He has been severely tortured."

"Is there anything you can do for him?" KiKu asked.

"No, but you can." Maura commanded KiKu, "Bring the amulet and place it around his neck."

KiKu did as bidden, looking expectantly at Maura. "Now what?"

"How is he?" asked Maura, looking to Meagan.

Meagan pressed an ear to Timon's chest and listened. "The beat is stronger, but far from being sound. You must help him."

"I cannot now. I must reserve all my strength," replied Maura, remembering Gitar's warning.

KiKu held out his hand. "He deserves to live."

Maura pulled her bed sheet over Timon. "Yes, he does, but unfortunately, we don't always receive the life we deserve. Isn't that what you taught me, KiKu? Life is not fair?

"Do not despair yet, my old friend. You are to take Timon and the amulet to his people in the steppes. They are north of here, almost at the foothills of the mountains. You will stay with him until I send for you."

"That is too arduous a trip for one as ill as this boy," burst out Meagan. She pointed at KiKu. "And this one is as weak as a newborn borax. No. No. No. I protest, Great Mother. I insist these two stay here and recover."

Meagan had pieced together from their whispers that Maura and KiKu had concocted a secret mission months ago, but now it was time for the subterfuge to stop. Enough was enough. Her patients must have rest.

Maura understood Meagan's concern. "I beg you,

listen. Have you not heard the pounding of the catapults all morning, Meagan of Skujpor? Do you not wonder as to why the west wall has not crumbled under such punishment?" Maura put a fresh, wet cloth on Timon's head and wiped his feverish brow. "I have. The wall and the gate should have been pulverized to rubble hours ago, but they stand as if nothing has touched them. That makes me suspect a spell surrounds the walls of the Bhuttani. Perhaps that is why the city has never been captured in a millennium."

"Magic?" Meagan asked.

Maura handed the bloodied cloth to the healer and answered, "We know the Bhuttanians used magic and kept wizards at court. Did not Dorak use magic to capture Hasan Daeg? I think the walls of Bhuttani will stand forever, especially if that amulet stays here. Perhaps, when it has left the vicinity, the spell surrounding the walls will weaken. It must go, and with it shall go our young friend, back to the north steppes of Moab. The amulet will help to keep our young Timon alive."

"Truly?" murmured Meagan, looking pitifully at Timon's struggles to breathe.

"I believe it will." Maura turned to KiKu. "I'm sorry, but you must leave immediately. You and Timon will be secreted in a laundry wagon as it proceeds to a stream, supposedly so my servants may do the wash. There a contingent of my warriors and provisions will meet you. They will take you to Timon's people, and there you shall remain until I summon you."

"My wives?"

"They will stay here under my protection."

Crestfallen, KiKu sputtered, "I want to see them. I have that right. I have done as you asked."

"That cannot happen. A large laundry wagon sent to the tent of your wives will have Mikkotto's spies following it."

"Put me in a cooking vessel and sneak me to them," KiKu begged.

"I forbid it. It's too risky. Every moment the amulet lingers near Bhuttani, it is a threat. It has served its purpose of freeing the Dinii. It must go, and you must take it away."

"Wait. Does it not provide invisibility? Did you not visit me wearing it, but unseen by all until you took it off. Bestow it upon me so that I may see my wives?"

"And what if Timon should die because he no longer wears the amulet while you go traipsing off to see your women? Is this what your stubbornness is about? You think I have killed your wives in a fit of pique because it took so long to free the Dinii?"

"My wives are alive? You swear to me?"

"They have a private tent and are in excellent health.

They have the best of everything—food, clothes, servants. I have given them everything to which women of their stature are entitled. You needn't worry."

"May I send them a message?"

"Give me a verbal one, and I will deliver personally, but nothing in writing."

"What if I write something down and you hand deliver it?"

"Should I be captured or killed and the scroll is found before I can deliver it puts their lives in danger. Very few people know they are here. Everyone thinks they have been banished. I take a risk as it is."

Frustrated, KiKu threw a bowl against the felt walls of the tent. "This is untenable. I want proof of life." He looked at Maura and could tell she was not going to relent. "Very well. Tell them I wish them good health, and I shall see them soon."

"You cut me to the quick with your mistrust, my old friend, but I will overlook it because you have been betrayed many times. I understand your suspicion, but I will do you a favor. I will elaborate on that message since you are too shy to relate your feelings about them."

"Feelings? My wives and I are not young people in love." KiKu hesitated. "I have only touched one of them as a man desires a woman."

"Why is that?" asked Meagan, curious.

"Because they were related to my family through either marriage or blood and left without a protector. I married my wives to safeguard them. They are educated and highborn. They represent my house well, and we take mutual care of each other. What else does a man need from a woman?"

Maura grinned. "I will add that you miss them."

"Harrumph," coughed KiKu, obviously embarrassed. It would not do for others to know that a spylord cared about anyone. That Meagan and Maura knew he worried about his wives might put them in more danger. Maura could use his concern as leverage, as she had done with the Bhuttanian generals. It was certainly a tactic Zoar used. Look at KiKu's poor sister, Mamora. Timon and his brother. Even KiKu himself.

Zoar ripped children from families to control opposing royal households. Now Maura was using the same method. The looming question was, would she release her "guests" after the war was over?

KiKu's stomach was queasy. Yes, he must be getting old to slip up so much. "What about Akela?"

"He is with them, safe and sound. Now you must hurry, KiKu. Take Timon to safety. My servants will take care of everything, but I must go now. I can't be too long from the front." Taking one last look at Timon lying prone and helpless in her bed, Maura called for three of the young Hasan Daegian lads who served her.

Taking them to a corner of the room, Maura gave explicit instructions about KiKu and Timon. They nodded, excited to be given such an important assignment, even though they had trained for every contingency.

In case their mission was compromised, they had been given lethal poison hidden behind their gums to use if captured by the enemy. Before they left, they would make sure KiKu and Timon each possessed the poison as well.

And they would use the poison if necessary without hesitation. All had pledged never to fail the Great Mother, daughter of the great Queen Abisola, who had freed them from servitude.

Yes, they would swallow the poison if they failed her.

To a man.

33

The Dinii made quick work.

They accomplished in several hours what would have taken Alexanee's soldiers days.

The forest had been picked clean. Only a few trees were left of what had been the lush royal hunting park for the great kings of Bhuttan. Now the gigantic trees were stacked as a mountain of logs and branches against the north wall of Bhuttani.

Alexanee ordered several catapults over to the north wall, realizing the west wall would never fall. But Alexanee still had the remaining catapults thumping great boulders against the west wall for he knew the noise alone was unsettling to those inside. He had to admit it was wearing on his nerves as well. Regardless of his personal discomfort, Alexanee had a job to do, and he would do it.

The north wall catapults were loaded with bundles of straw, twigs, and dried borax droppings, which the cooks used for fuel.

Alexanee tested the wind. It was in his favor and blowing from northwest to southeast. He was sure the stench of the many borax arse biscuits would waft throughout the city. To cause further distress, he ordered fresh borax droppings loaded into catapult buckets as well.

None of the Hasan Daegians and Anqarians assigned to the north wall complained of pushing wheelbarrows of pungent fresh droppings to the north wall. If this would hasten the end of the siege, they were happy to oblige.

Great ewers of oil were smashed against the mountain of timber, saturating the logs and making them more flammable.

Mikkotto did everything she could to counter Alexanee's maneuvers. She was reluctant to use precious reserves of water since Alexanee had now cut off the city's supply as predicted, but she could not have foreseen the return of the Dinii, who accelerated the building the dam. Having no other choice, Mikkotto ordered great vats of water to be poured over the great heaps of logs, making it harder to ignite the incendiary material below.

Seeing that Alexanee ordered more containers of oil, Mikkotto rescinded her command to drench the pile of logs. Instead, she directed her troops to hurl sand over the walls to impede the outbreak of fire.

Worried that the sand might inhibit the ignition of the wood, Alexanee ordered the lighting of the logs.

Twenty Hasan Daegian archers targeted the mound of wood and let loose flaming arrows. Every one found its mark.

A great conflagration sprang forth like a wild beast that had been coiled for attack. The fire enveloped its prey—snarling, spitting, and ripping. Flames shot above the ramparts, pushing back the Bhuttanians trying to put the fire out.

Alexanee heard the screams of Bhuttanian soldiers, whose sleeves or tunics had caught on fire and were now engulfed in flames.

Men became flaming torches and fell over the wall into the inferno, their screams striking fear into those working on the catapults and the river dam.

Alexanee wanted to look away but couldn't. He had to remain strong for the soldiers under his command, but he was sickened as they were.

Why didn't Jezra or her commander, Mikkotto, put an end to this carnage and open the west gate?

Would Maura be forced to undertake a full-scale

annihilation in order to take the city?

He knew the Bhuttanians under his command would never stand for it. There would likely be open rebellion among his men if they didn't conquer the city before nightfall.

That wall had to give way—and soon!

34

The battle was in full force.

Maura ordered the catapults from the west wall moved to the north wall.

The Dinii, each one ten times stronger than any man in Maura's army, made quick work of moving the heavy machines.

While the catapults were relocated, she ordered a male contingent of Hasan Daegian archers to continually harass the remaining soldiers on the west wall.

The Bhuttanians fought bravely, but they were not prepared for the sheer number of arrows flying over the battlements.

Many a rebel warrior was struck down by a Hasan Daegian arrow piercing his neck and spurting his life's blood on his comrade.

Confident the north wall would hold, Mikkotto ordered the surviving soldiers to collect the Hasan Daegian arrows, even if it meant pulling them out of a comrade's flesh.

She knew Maura would soon order troops to deploy ladders to the west wall. In anticipation, she prepared a little surprise for her cousin.

Exhausted but determined, Mikkotto wiped the grime of battle off her face. A fresh shower of arrows rained down upon her men. Taking cover, she ducked into a stone guardhouse, cursing Abisola for giving rights to Hasan Daegian males. Who knew the dainty men of her country would be such deadly archers?

When Mikkotto became queen of Hasan Daeg, she would undo this travesty. No rights for the males—back to domestic life where they belonged.

Mikkotto had many things to set right, but she had to win this war to accomplish them. She assessed that the city was holding its own against the invaders, but it was not winning. She had to find something or someone who would help turn the tide against Maura. If Mikkotto could somehow eliminate the Blue Witch, the renegade Bhuttanians would rejoin their brethren within the city walls.

Maura must die—but how? Every assassin she sent to terminate Maura failed. Poisoned darts, poisoned food, poisoned water, or hired mercenaries with sharp blades had all come to naught. She had even enlisted her own child to kill Maura, but nothing came of it but a dead son.

Perhaps she was concentrating too much on paid assassins. She still had many supporters in Maura's camp, especially among the nobility, who disliked Queen Abisola's reforms.

And Mikkotto knew from her spies that a growing number of Bhuttanian generals were disgruntled. Only Alexanee's stern discipline kept them in line—and the fact that the generals' families were secluded in a camp on the east side of the city guarded by Hasan Daegian women.

Perhaps if she sent a contingent of soldiers to release the generals' families, they would not be so inclined to serve the usurper, Maura.

Hmm, that was a thought.

35

The city was on fire.

Winds from the plains carried embers to rooftops, scattering the flames.

Mikkotto and her soldiers fought bravely to contain the inferno, but the fire was too strong, and the heat drove them off. Soon all the buildings near the north wall were alight.

Mikkotto ordered her soldiers away, realizing that even if the wall gave way, the smoldering rubble would be too hot for Maura's forces to cross.

It would take days and even weeks for the debris to cool, and her soldiers would have established a foothold in that section by then.

Mikkotto was positive the fire was a diversion to draw soldiers away from the west side of the city, which was where she convinced the main attack would happen. She ordered her men back to the west wall again. As they hurried across the city, the men collected thousands of Hasan Daegian arrows and threw them into carts to be reissued to other soldiers.

Chuckling, Mikkotto muttered, "Thank you, Maura, for replenishing our munitions. We were low on arrows, and you solved our problem. We will happily send them back to you, hopefully landing in the chest of one of your darling archer boys."

Returning to the task at hand, she yelled from the battlements. "Is this all you've got? The wall stands. Bhuttani is unvanquished. The Aganess Jezra is still queen.

"You puny little Hasan Daegian men. When I'm queen, you will all go back to the kitchens where you belong."

An arrow whizzed past her cheek. Mikkotto felt her face and saw blood on her fingers. "So, you've drawn blood, you creatures of Maura. I will have my revenge on you all," Mikkotto cursed. "I will. I swear I will. Even to my last breath."

36

Maura sat atop Dorak's steed.

Alexanee rode beside her, his mount pawing the ground impatiently. He shouted against the roar of the fire. "Mikkotto has moved her men back to the west gate. The north wall is white hot. We need to strike now."

"She's not fighting the fire?" Maura asked.

"With what? She must preserve what little water she has. And the fire burns too hot for her men to get close enough to throw sand."

Maura agreed. "That leaves this wall wide open. Now is the time to strike. Give the order to break the dam."

Alexander waved a purple flag as his nervous horse pranced to and from the embankment of the water canal.

The trumpeter sounded the signal to open the dam.

Engineers on either side of the river cut ropes holding logs in place. As the logs tumbled into the water, the river surged forward. A tall wave of water littered with debris, including rotting bodies of both people and animals, rushed into the canal bed, overflowing its banks. The wave consumed everything in its path, engulfing the raging fire at the base of the wall.

Maura and Alexanee watched expectantly, knowing this was their one chance to breach the walls of Bhuttani. Would the cold water against the hot stones cause the wall to crack?

Alexanee peered through his field glass as the other Bhuttanian generals rode up from behind Maura and Alexanee, encircling them.

Maura unsheathed her sword, knowing this was where the Bhuttanian Generals planned to make their stand against her. They were furious that Bhuttani was on fire.

Sensing danger, the uultepes by her side turned and growled.

Maura would be hard to kill, but she was still mortal, and surviving against ten battle-hardened men attacking her at once would be difficult, even with the uultepes by her side.

Anticipating that the Bhuttanian generals would

strike, Maura had ordered her guards to watch over Dyanna, for the generals surely would send men to kill her daughter at the same time they attacked her. But they didn't know Maura had removed Dyanna from the royal tent and placed her in the care of Empress Gitar. If they received word of Maura's death, Gitar and the Dinii would fly away, taking Dyanna to safety with them.

Taking a deep breath, Maura was readying her sword to strike when Alexanee rose up in his saddle.

"Do you hear it? Do you hear it?" he cried out, handing the field glass to Maura. He pointed toward the wall. "Look. Look!"

Maura looked through the lens, the skin on her neck crawling, since she expected this might be a ploy to get her guard down.

"Don't you hear it, Great Mother?"

"I hear the hissing of the water against the rocks."

"Under that. Don't you hear a rumbling?"

Maura strained to listen. Something significant did seem to be happening. "We need to take a closer look."

She untied the strap of the shield wrapped around her saddle horn and urged her horse forward.

Water roiled against blistering stones and plaster, creating a cloud of steam.

Alexanee reached over and caught her horse's bridle.

"You mustn't. It's too dangerous."

"I can't see what's happening, which means Mikkot-to can't see either. Believe me when I say she's watching."

"All the more reason for you not to go nearer."

"Let go of my horse, General. I'd rather die by a Bhuttanian arrow to my chest than a Bhuttanian sword to my back."

Realizing Maura's meaning, Alexanee snapped his attention to the generals surrounding them. Acting unconcerned, he ordered a younger general, "You, there. Take a closer look."

The young general glanced at his comrades before urging his horse forward.

In that brief moment, it was obvious that Alexanee was not going to support any attempt to kill Maura, and would stand against them. If they acted, they would have to kill him as well, but the rest of the generals did not make their move, recalculating their strategy. They had not taken into account that Alexanee would stand with the blue witch.

Reluctantly, the young general rode into the blanket of smoke and embers.

Maura held her breath until he emerged again, steam rising off his armor and warhorse.

He paused before the queen and the knot of generals. "There is a continuous crack going from the base to the top, but the wall still stands."

Maura spoke, "General, identify the position of the fracture and direct the catapults against its location."

"No."

"No?" echoed Maura. "We have a chance to break down this wall."

"The wall will never fall. It will not rupture. It will hold fast until we squander every resource at our disposal and exhaust every man and woman in our army."

"Obey your empress!" ordered Alexanee, turning his horse to face the band of generals. He feared the moment of reckoning had finally come. The Bhuttanian generals under his command were making their move.

"Think about your families, men!" Maura cautioned.

"Indeed, we have, my lady," replied the most senior of the generals. "We have sent troops to the refugee camp to rescue them. All your Hasan Daegian guards are dead, and our families have been set free, along with the rest of our people you have held in confinement. Once we receive word our families are unharmed, we will give the signal to our troops to switch their loyalty and begin fighting against you, Blue Witch."

"My good generals. I'm afraid you have overplayed your hand."

Fear and distrust crept into the generals' eyes.

"Your families are not in the refugee camps. They are secured in Hasan Daeg."

"That can't be. Hasan Daeg is thousands of miles away."

"That is correct, and that is where your families are. I knew you would switch loyalties . . . again. I had many of your families rounded up and sent to Hasan Daeg."

"She's bluffing!" came a voice from the group of generals.

"Am I?"

"There's no way you could capture our families."

"You forget. Members of your family travel. They have business in other cities. You all have summer homes on the river where the families congregate during the worst heat. It was nothing to send special units disguised as Bhuttanians and capture a family member here and there, especially sons. According to my reports, we captured most of your sons, since Bhuttanians have such high regard for their male heirs."

"Our sons are in this army fighting beside us."

Maura looked around. "They are? Where? You will not find them because my women rounded them up this morning."

A general rushed Maura, whereupon a uultepe leapt up and knocked the general off his saddle, then crouching over him, his head in her mouth.

"Stand down," Maura cautioned the other generals. "My uultepe's automatic response is to close her jaw. She would crush this man's head like a melon without meaning to."

Maura cooed to her uultepe. "Let the man sit up, my pet." She looked down at the fallen general. "Xizing, isn't it? You have a grown daughter by your first wife and an infant son with your second wife, who I think is the daughter of . . ." Maura hesitated and pointed at another general. "A daughter of yours, General Ju Li. In fact, she is your favorite daughter. They are in my custody and safe. They were on their way to meet you both several months ago when my warriors intercepted them and started them on their journey to Hasan Daeg."

General Ju Li protested, "You lie. They could not join us because illness prevented them, but we both have been receiving missives from them, even recently as several days ago."

"Yes, I know about those letters. My people began intercepting your letters several years ago. In fact, all letters written by you have been decoded by my scribes, who took the liberty of writing back to your families in your name. And letters from your families were written by my scribes as well.

"As for the refugee camp? Well, your men will find an empty camp with only a few smoldering campfires. But you are right, I could be lying. Your families could be hidden nearby, and if I fall to your swords, my guards have been ordered to slaughter them."

The Bhuttanian generals looked dumbfounded.

General Ju Li bowed. "Empress Maura, you have bested us. We underestimated your cunning. We will fight to the death on your behalf, if you promise to honor the safety of our families." Alexanee, bitter at this betrayal, snarled, "Get back to your posts, men, or I swear I'll have you hung for this."

General Xizing argued, "You'll have us hung anyway. Our families are good as dead. Let's kill them both now."

"Kill them. Kill them. Kill them," chanted the other generals.

General Ju Li pulled out his sword and pointed it at the other generals. "What are you doing? She promised our families are safe. Stop, I tell you. Stop!"

Maura looked around. She was on her own, because she had sent her guards to protect Princess Dyanna. She was not sure which side Alexanee would choose at the last moment.

The other generals pushed General Ju Li aside, and were tightening the circle to attack when suddenly a pulsating orange light passed through the group, catching one general in its beam. The general and his horse were burned to a crisp without a single cry from either man or beast.

Confused, the generals pulled their horses back.

What was this!

Alexanee shot a look at Maura. She seemed as surprised as he.

Maura cried, "Look! The beam is aimed against the crack in the wall."

A courier pushed through the circle of neighing and stomping warhorses, dodging under the beam of pulsating light, and ran up to Maura. "Great Mother," she cried, excitedly handing over a scroll. "The river! The river!"

Maura broke the seal and read quickly.

"What is it?" asked Alexanee, noting that Maura's face had drained of color.

Looking at Alexanee, Maura crushed the message, throwing it on the ground. "We have won! We have won! The city is ours!" Spurring her horse, she pushed through the knot of generals and galloped to the river.

Alexanee had the courier retrieve the message and hand it to him. He read it slowly.

"Well?" asked the surviving generals.

"It's in a language I have never seen before. I can't

decipher it. Whatever it is, our empress knew what it meant, and that's why she's heading toward the river. That's where this beam is coming from, and where the answer lies."

Alexanee folded the message and secured it in his tunic. "Go back to your posts, generals. You have lost your bid for freedom. You are Maura's creatures yet. Direct these catapults to fire directly where that beam hits the wall.

"And men, I tell you this. If one hair on Princess Dyanna's head is mussed, I will skin each and every one of you alive myself, but not before I do the same to your sons and make you watch."

Furious, but realizing they had been outmaneuvered, the generals headed back to their posts, with one general rushing to call off his men sent to assassinate Princess Dyanna. Two others raced for the river. They wanted to determine the source of the magical orange beam of light.

Everyone was in disarray and confusion. The sky above the river had turned dark with Dinii hovering above, shouting, hooting, hissing, and obviously threatened. The Dinii's distress caused a great deal of concern among the troops congregating near the river. Discipline among the soldiers collapsed as the frightened soldiers argued among themselves.

Some were pushed into the intense beam and were burned while officers struggled to restore order and avert a full-scale riot.

Maura heard Iegani calling to her in her mind, "Maura, hurry. Hurry to the river!"

Maura spurred her horse through the mob of soldiers until heralds ran in front of her, trumpeting the empress's arrival. "Make way! Make way! The Great Mother is coming!"

The trumpets and cries of heralds caused the hordes in front of Maura to bow and clear a pathway. Behind her warhorse, commanders ran with whips and barked threats, ordering their soldiers back to their positions, but no one moved.

Maura's horse, sensing the tension in the air, grew skittish and reared high off the ground until Maura urged him forward.

As Maura neared the riverbank, she saw Empress Gitar in a palanquin with Iegani and Chaun Maaun close behind, all hurrying to the source of the pulsating beam.

"Out of my way!" yelled Maura to her troops as she urged her horse to a fast trot.

She and Gitar reached the river at the same time.

Maura couldn't believe the sight that greeted her.

Over the still-swirling waters of the flooded river were more than a hundred spheres of varied sizes and every color imaginable. The Lahorians!

"They've come!" cried Maura, stunned. If the Lahorians were here, it meant they had determined she would fail without their intervention.

Fear clutched Maura's heart. She tried to rationalize their abrupt appearance. Perhaps they had planned to intercede all along.

She jumped off the horse and sprinted into the water until waist deep.

Gitar's bearers also splashed into the water, accompanied by Chaun Maaun and Iegani.

Dinii warriors swooped from the sky and formed a barrier between the empresses and the multitude of soldiers, servants, cooks, and farriers who had rushed to the water to watch. Many took to wagons and even climbed upon one another's shoulders to witness what was happening.

Maura walked farther into the river until the water rippled up to her chest.

One of the orbs opened, and a naked man emerged. Maura could see his internal organs pulsing beneath his translucent skin. He flicked his wrist, and the river's murky brown water receded from around Gitar and Maura. "Do not come closer, Great Ladies. I will come to you."

With another flip of his hand, a wave carried him

forward until he was only a few feet from the empresses.

Other spheres opened, revealing more Lahorians.

Both Maura and Gitar inclined their heads, for they realized they stood before the real rulers of the planet Kaseri.

"Greeting, Lords of the Water," said Maura. "We welcome you."

"Empress of the Dinii, please tell your people to calm themselves. We are here only to assist."

"They recognize ancient enemies."

"We are enemies no longer, since our treaty regarding Abisola's conception of Maura. Tell them to stand down. They must not breach the orbs with their talons."

Gitar nodded to Iegani, who sent a mental message to all the Dinii hovering in the air above the Lahorians. The Dinii flew off and settled along the riverbanks.

"I only have a few moments to speak with you. You cannot break down Bhuttani's walls without us. Do not interfere. Do not touch us. We are one. We are one."

The man flicked his hand again, and a wave carried him back to his orb, which immediately closed around him. Water rushed forward, surrounding Gitar and Maura, and they made haste to escape the disturbed river now lapping angrily against its banks.

"Get your people ready, Empress," shouted Maura

over the din of her troops. "We attack soon." She jumped on her steed and waved her sword high above her head. "Back to your positions. We attack upon my signal," she cried, rallying her forces. "We shall put an end to this war, once and for all!"

37

Mikkotto raced to the north wall.

A beam of pulsating light was searing through the thick stones of the wall.

Maura's foot soldiers, archers, and cavalry stood between the river and the city, waiting for the wall to crumble, and portable bridges, to be placed over the hot debris, were pulled from the river by the Dinii. The waterlogged wood would not catch fire, and thus would provide a way for soldiers to march into Bhuttani once the wall gave way.

Mikkotto marveled at the power of a ray of light that could cut through stone. From whence did it come? Did Maura have wizards now?

A lieutenant rushed up to Mikkotto.

"What news have you?"

"All archers have assembled at the west gate."

"News from Maura's Bhuttanian generals?"

"They are standing firm with the usurper. They have not swayed."

Mikkotto waved the lieutenant away. She did not want him to see the anxiety in her eyes. Once Maura breached the walls, Mikkotto's soldiers would likely falter. The war would be lost. She motioned to one of her warriors and whispered, "Have a swift horse waiting for me at the south gate."

"There are no more horses, Baroness. You commandeered all the horses for the army."

"Then steal the best one you can find."

The guard shook her head. "The army has eaten them. There are no more horses. Besides, you ordered the south gate barricaded. It would take hours, if not days, to remove the debris."

Mikkotto's greatest fear was realized. The north wall would soon give way.

Was there nothing that could save her and the city?

38

*Z*edek awakened.

Sensing a disturbance in the magic he had cast, Zedek sniffed the smoky air and waved his bony hand in front of his face. The spells throughout the city were in flux. Something was happening to interfere with his enchantments.

Zedek roared. Jumping out of his bed deep in the bowels of the palace, he raced to the rooftop, cursing the fact that he no longer had the amulet. At least it was safe under the piles of rubble that had been the temple of Bhuttu. There it would remain until he could retrieve it.

Zedek forgot about the amulet when he spied a beam of yellowish-orange light pulsating from the direction of the river. Zedek could feel his magic weakening. The wall was going to give way, and much of the city was either on fire or smoldering. How could this be?

Furious at being bested, Zedek drew himself up and, using all his hate and anger, changed into a mighty dragon. Screeching a terrible cry, the dragon leapt from the roof and swooped down upon the very heart of Maura's army. If fire was what that damned bitch Maura wanted, then fire she would have. The dragon took a deep breath and exhaled a blaze of fire so blistering, it turned sand on the ground into bits of glass.

Soldiers scattered, trying to find cover from the dragon's barrage of fire, but entire squads were burned beyond recognition.

Maura rode her horse into the river. "Direct your beam upon the dragon!" she cried out to the Lahorians. "Kill the dragon!"

The Lahorians ignored Maura and continued directing their beam of energy at the wall.

Realizing the Lahorians were disregarding her commands, Maura charged the fearsome dragon, screaming, "Chaun Maaun. Kill the dragon! Kill the dragon!"

Stunned, the Dinii remained on the opposite side of the river. They had never seen a dragon, much less encountered a flying creature that breathed fire. Confused, they glanced around, not knowing what to do.

Seeing the Dinii unfurl their wings, Maura grasped that the Dinii would dart up into the sky and hover above the clouds until they felt safe. If that happened, all would be lost.

Yesemek and Yeti shouted to their Dinii comrades, "Stand your ground. HOLD FAST!"

Maura turned her horse around and found Chaun Maaun close behind her, lounging against a broken-down wagon, watching the dragon, unfazed. She kicked her mount toward him. "Give the order to attack, Chaun Maaun. We must kill that dragon."

"So that's what it is."

"Don't be a fool," Maura screamed.

"Would you be willing to die to kill it, Maura?"

Without hesitation, Maura snapped, "Yes! Hurry, before the dragon destroys both our peoples. Hurry!"

"Beg me."

Astonished, Maura blinked. "Have you gone mad? Your hatred of me runs so deep that you would let our people die simply to thwart me?" She glanced over her shoulder to see the dragon swooping toward her troops, who were rushing to the river. "I'm begging you, Prince Chaun Maaun of the Dinii. Save us. Save my people. Save the Dinii. Save me."

Chaun Maaun unfurled his wings and fluttered, motioning to Maura to climb on his back. She jumped from her nervous warhorse onto Chaun Maaun's back as she had done hundreds of times before, and held on with one hand while brandishing her sword with the other.

The Dinii prince shot into the air and circled his warriors. "Grab a soldier and follow me!" he cried.

One by one, Dinii warriors lowered themselves into the water, allowing drenched and terrified soldiers to climb on their backs before vaulting into the air. A few soldiers fell back into the river. Others, who had the sense to hang on, were flown into the smoke-filled sky screaming cries of the horrified, the determined, and the damned.

39

Soldiers rushed to the north wall.

They helped the dragon annihilate Maura's army, leaving the palace unprotected. Bhuttanian scum saw the opportunity to plunder the Imperial Palace of every last bit of metal, coin, tapestry, utensils, food, drink, oil, and candles they could lay their hands on.

Seizing the opportunity, Dorak found it easy to enter the palace and, ignoring the looters, hurried upstairs. Calling out Jezra's name, he went first to the nursery but found no one. Hastening to Jezra's chambers, he passed his mother's old suite. The door was off its hinges, and inside women were pawing through his mother's clothes. Aghast, Dorak thought about killing the thieves. But no. He needed to find Jezra and his son. Time was running out.

Arriving at Jezra's apartments, he tried the massive

wooden door. It was locked. "Jezra. Jezra. Open the door. It's Dorak!"

Dorak heard a faint click and pulled out his dagger, not knowing what awaited him on the other side. The door opened a bit as a servant woman peered out. Upon seeing Dorak, she exclaimed, "Lady, it is your husband. It's Lord Dorak!"

"Lock the door, you idiot."

"But my lady," protested the servant, doubt clouding her eyes.

Upon hearing Jezra speak, Dorak burst through the door and pushed the servant aside, locking the door behind him. "Jezra, it is I, Dorak. Don't you realize the palace is under attack? We must make haste from here."

"Shall I go with you so you can slit my throat? Why aren't you dead? I thought surely Maura had done away with you." Jezra grabbed her frightened son and clutched him tightly while she slowly inched towards the balcony.

Dorak shot a look of disbelief at the servant, who shook her head at him.

Taking a further step into the room, Dorak said, "I will give you my dagger, Jezra. I only want to take you and our son away from here, to somewhere you both will be safe." He placed the dagger on a table.

"So you can hand us over to Maura?" scoffed Jezra.

"No, my wife. I am no longer in league with Maura. You must believe me."

"Why should I, after you abandoned your son and me for that blue witch?"

Dorak put his hands out in supplication. "Jezra, come to me. We can escape through a secret tunnel in the dungeon."

Jezra squeezed the child in her arms more tightly until he burst into tears, squirming to be free.

"You would like us in the dungeon, wouldn't you, so you can enthrone your Hasan Daegian whore in my place. Then her bastard child would inherit the throne."

"No, Jezra. I'm trying to save you and our son. You can't stay here. We will flee together to the land below Siva, where we can hide from Maura."

"You'd leave the throne of your father? You expect me to believe that you will leave Bhuttan?"

"I have lost the throne to Maura. She will never take me back. I either escape with you or face her wrath."

"I saw a dragon circling in the sky. It is Zedek. He will never let her win. He will crush her. Then you will sit upon the throne again, but this time I will be by your side."

"Jezra, it is over. We have gambled and lost. There is no way a single dragon can defeat thousands of Dinii. They will fall upon him as Sivans upon a borax corpse. Bhuttan will be absorbed into Maura's new order. Jezra,

Maura has won."

Jezra's cornflower blue eyes grew moist as she stepped out onto the balcony. "Then all truly is lost. All is lost . . . lost," she said, looking over the railing.

"My lady," cautioned the servant. "Please come back into the room. You or your son might be injured by a stray arrow."

"Jezra, back away from the railing," Dorak ordered in his harshest commander's voice. "Come with me. We can start over."

"My son will never sit upon his grandfather's throne. He will never be the Great Aga, Lord of the Bhuttanian Empire. You have seen to that—you and your father!"

Dorak inched closer to Jezra, calculating the distance between them before he rushed the balcony.

Seeing his intention, Jezra turned and hurled her son over the railing.

Dorak froze in terror at the sound of his son's screams as he fell. Then the sound of a thud and silence.

Jezra cast Dorak a sweet smile before leaning over the railing and plunging headfirst to the cobblestones below.

Dorak and the servant rushed to the balustrade and peered over.

Looters swarmed the cobblestone courtyard, surrounding Jezra and tearing jewelry and hair ornaments off her twitching body. Seeing she was still alive, one of the looters viciously stomped on her head. The twitching stopped.

Beside her lay the body of her son, whose unseeing eyes stared at the sky.

Dorak groaned.

"Sire, you must hurry. Time is precious, and you can do no more for those poor, wretched beings."

Dorak stared at the servant in disbelief.

"Sire, her mind was never strong, and at the end was completely gone. Even if you had gotten out of the palace with them, you would have had to kill her eventually."

"But the boy? My son?"

"He was as she. He would never have been capable of ruling. Now you must flee, with utmost haste."

"What of you, good lady?"

"I will follow my mistress. My life was dedicated to her service. It is my choice. Now go, and leave this wicked place."

Dorak retrieved his dagger from the table and hurried into the hallway, where he blended in with the looters and made his way down to the dungeon. Finding several forgotten prisoners, he set them free and, once they left, Dorak collapsed upon a battered stool and wept. He wept for Jezra, his son, his father Zoar, and Maura. But most of all he wept for himself.

40

Chaun Maaun soared high above the cloud cover. The Dinii followed. "Hang on," he shouted.

Maura tightened her legs and strengthened her grip on the sword.

The prince shot down through the clouds like an avenging demon, his talons extended. Hundreds of Dinii followed, flying in formation until the city was in view again.

Hearing a piercing roar, Maura peered upward.

The dragon was high above, making straight for the Dinii. The Dinii scattered like a flock of crows, realizing they had made a serious tactical error.

The dragon streaked after them, opened its mouth and shot out flames, instantly killing scores of Dinii and their passenger soldiers. They fell burning to the ground.

For a brief second, Maura turned away, horrified at the sight of so many falling to their deaths. Others screamed when their feathers were so badly scorched they could not sustain flight, and they too plummeted from the sky.

Chaun Maaun roared, "Take evasive action."

Those who could regrouped.

Maura looked back and saw the dragon veer to the river and unleash fire upon the clustered Lahorians. As the wind blew the smoke and burning embers away, Maura saw scores of Lahorian spheres charred beyond recognition.

Hasan Daegian archers rushed to the river and fired arrows into the sky, many of them finding their mark in the thick, scaly hide of the dragon. Angry at being struck, the dragon bore down on the archers, who had the good sense to rush into the river and duck underwater. Those who survived the dragon's blast leapt up and fired again, but their arrows were torched mid-flight by another fireball. The archers ducked under the water again, only to re-emerge with their bows loaded and let loose another barrage of arrows.

As the archers distracted the dragon, a new contingent of Dinii, headed by Yesemek, attacked the fearsome beast from behind.

The dragon snapped its head around in anger.

Seeing his chance, Chaun Maaun dove under the dragon's exposed neck and sliced its slimy green skin with his talons while Maura hacked with her sword. Other Dinii followed, flying under the dragon's belly so their human companions could slash at the creature's most vulnerable parts.

Besieged on all sides, the dragon roared and, with a flip of his tail, knocked Yesemek and many of her warriors senseless. As they fell unconscious through the sky, other Dinii flew to their rescue and caught them. Burdened with soldiers on their backs and holding wounded comrades in their arms, these Dinii had no choice but to retreat.

Chaun Maaun came to rest near the catapults, letting Maura jump off.

"Where is he?" she cried, regarding the sky with a livid glare.

"Maura, you're on fire!" muttered Chaun Maaun, slapping the flames out on Maura's back. Indeed, Maura's face was burned on her right side, and her uniform smoldered.

A Hasan Daegian water girl, seeing Maura with Chaun Maaun trying to beat out the fire, ran over and threw a bucket of water on her.

Maura turned to thank her as the lass took an arrow in the back. Grabbing the girl as she fell, Maura lay her motionless on the ground and gently closed her eyes.

Alexanee ran over to Maura. "Look, the wall is starting to crumble."

Maura could barely hear him over the tumult of the catapults. Her gaze followed his outstretched arm to the wall where the Lahorians had concentrated their destructive ray of light. "Hit it!" she bellowed. "Hit it hard!"

A great cry pierced the sky. Everyone ducked as a shadow passed across the ground.

Maura stood up, screaming, "Keep the catapults going! That wall must come down."

The dragon circled the city and landed on the ramparts, launching a stream of fiery retribution at the catapults, which burst into flames like dried-out shocks of fodder after a fall harvest. The dragon then flew to the ground where he tossed petrified soldiers into the air while stomping on others. There was utter chaos among Maura's foot soldiers as they fled for their lives.

Maura grabbed Chaun Maaun's hand. "Take me to him. This must end."

Nodding, Chaun Maaun picked Maura up in his arms and flew to the left of the dragon while the Dinii flanked the dragon on the right.

Chaun Maaun looked questioningly at Maura.

She nodded.

He let go.

Years of training had prepared her to fall skillfully. Somersaulting in midair, Maura pointed her sword downward so she would land feet-first and drive her sword into the dragon's neck.

Crashing into the back of the dragon, Maura's feet went out from under her, and she slid across its oily scales, landing next to its feet. Maura rolled underneath the dragon, which was now beset by the Dinii striking behind its head.

Furious, the dragon bellowed, snapping at the Dinii and belching great waves of fire, but the Dinii were too quick for him now. Like all born predators, they quickly learned the dragon's abilities and weaknesses, adapting their skills to combat it.

Maura recognized many of the Dinii's cries—Chaun Maaun, Yeti, Benzar, and Tarsus were just a few of the Dinii battling the great behemoth, giving Maura the time she needed. She moved to the part of the dragon's chest where scales didn't cover the skin as densely. She plunged her sword into the dragon's breast as far as she could, thrusting through the thick reptilian skin.

The dragon halted, then staggered and lurched forward.

Maura ran until Alexanee caught her. Behind him marched several squads of Hasan Daegian women, ready to pounce upon the beast. "Be still, Empress. You are safe."

Blinded by the smoke and ash, Maura grabbed Alexanee's arm and steadied herself. "Give me your sword. I must finish this."

"The dragon is severely wounded. The Dinii can dispatch it. You must see a healer. Your eyes are damaged."

"I'll heal myself. Give me your sword." Maura seized Alexanee's sword and made her way back to the dragon, which was now stumbling around, desperately trying to pull out the Aga's sword.

Seeing Maura make way for the dragon again, Chaun Maaun flew over and silently whisked her up into his arms.

Maura made not a sound as they landed on the back of the dragon. Chaun Maaun guided Maura's hands upon the hilt of the sword, and together they plunged it into the base of the dragon's skull.

The dragon breathed one last cry and staggered, shuddering, until it came crashing down.

The Dinii descended upon the dragon, rending its flesh and eating it with such a fury that Alexanee turned away in disgust. The Hasan Daegians broke rank and rushed the dragon, stabbing it with their pikes and daggers.

Chaun Maaun flew to the river and bathed Maura's eyes, although the debris floating in the river made it hard to scoop up clean water.

Metal clanging against metal reverberated over the din of soldiers whooping and hollering.

"What's happening? What's that noise?" asked Maura, straining to see.

"The Lahorians are leaving. Iegani is having our people push their spheres into deeper water."

Maura struggled to get up. "Is he mad? They can't leave."

Chaun Maaun grabbed her and spun her around to face Bhuttani. "Maura, can't you see? The wall is crumbling. It's coming down!"

"Chaun Maaun, help me stand. I can't make it on my own."

Alarmed, Chaun Maaun helped Maura stand, noticing that she was holding her side. "What's this? You're bleeding."

"Be still," she commanded. "Help me bind my wound before anyone notices."

Chaun Maaun reached and pulled over a dead soldier floating in the water. Tearing off part of the soldier's tunic, he wrapped the cloth around Maura's midsection and bound her wound.

"Look fast. Alexanee is approaching."

Alexanee rode up to the couple with Maura's war-horse in tow. "Empress, the north wall has crumbled, and the west gate is demolished. We await your word to enter the city."

Maura mounted Dorak's steed.

Alexanee handed the reins to her.

"General Alexanee, give the signal to enter the city and clear my path to the Bhuttanian throne."

Alexanee nodded to a bugler.

Upon hearing the signal, archers let loose a flurry of arrows with red ribbons. Hasan Daegians, Camaroons, Hittals, Anqarians, Bhuttanians, and a multitude of mercenaries from other nations marched into Bhuttani while the Dinii flew overhead and came to rest on rooftops across the city.

Maura's army was met with little resistance. Word had spread throughout the city that Jezra and her son were dead, as was the great dragon. The city was on fire. The people of Bhuttani were resigned to their fate. Once the terror of Kaseri, the Bhuttanians were now the defeated.

The war was over!

41

The empress opened court.

Maura, wearing the State Robes of the Aga, held both the Royal Fan of Hasan Daeg signifying her station as queen and the Sword of the Aga signifying her station as dowager aganess. A step higher on the dais sat the assembled Dinii royalty—Gitar, Iegani, and Chaun Maaun. A step below Maura stood a nurse holding Princess Dyanna.

Yeti, Toppo, and Benzar stood guard in front of the dais, doing their best to hide their grief. Tarsus was no more, burned to death by Zedek's dragon.

Maura studied the people congregating in the great hall of the Imperial Palace, which stank of smoke and blood. Filthy from battle, her generals watched the proceedings, as well as high-ranking Dinii and Hasan Daegian officers, priestesses from the House of Magi, and anyone else who could squeeze in the hall.

Bhuttanian noblemen, quaking with fear, were pushed to the front of the dais and made to kowtow. The scent of fear aroused the uultepes, which prowled around, nipping here and there for good measure.

A squad of soldiers pushed through the crowd, delivering KiKu's wives to a vantage point in the great hall. Saluting to Maura, they left the women and returned to their stations.

Madric, Tippu, Tippa, and Pearl glanced around. Pearl, clutching Akela's hand, grinned at the kowtowing Bhuttanian nobles. She enjoyed their humiliation.

Akela tugged on Pearl's skirt. "There's that blue lady. Is she our new king?"

"Quiet, Akela. Watch and remember. This is an auspicious day. You will regale your great-grandchildren with tales of it."

Akela frowned. Great-grandchildren? What silly notions Mistress Pearl had at times.

Maura leaned forward and pointed her fan at the quivering nobles. "Were not most of you at my wedding to Aga Dorak, and saw me crowned as Empress of the Bhuttanian Empire?"

The nobles bobbed their heads.

"Why do you shake? Have you committed a crime? Should I be displeased with something you have done?"

The nobles shook their heads.

"Why were the gates of Bhuttani closed to me, your ruling empress?"

One noble lifted his head to explain. "Empress, the first wife of Dorak, Jezra, forbade it. She said you had murdered Aga Dorak and your crown should be forfeited in favor of her son."

"Did she provide you with proof of my supposed heinous deed?"

A strained silence ensued until a lone voice spoke up, "No, Empress."

"Do you even know if Aga Dorak is deceased?"

"No, Empress."

"Where is Aga Dorak, then?" yelled someone from the crowd.

Maura answered without hesitating in a booming voice that filled the hall. "Aga Dorak was caught in a spell brought on by his own wizard Zedek. For years, the cursed wizard Zedek and a band of my Dinii comrades languished with Dorak in the temple of Bhuttu, unable to inform the outside world of their whereabouts. It is believed that Aga Dorak died when the temple fell as a result of more spell-weaving by his wizard. We are looking through the rubble for his remains now."

The couturiers muttered among themselves while

Maura's Bhuttanian generals puffed themselves up for being on the winning side, their aborted act of regicide entirely forgotten—by then.

Maura gestured for the court to be quiet. "You took up arms against me without proof. On nothing more than the word of a young woman whose mind was unsettled."

"Forgive us, Empress," they begged in unison. "Forgive us."

Maura stood upright and pointed her fan at them. "I forgive nothing. You had no authority to keep the gates of Bhuttani closed to me. Your treasonous actions have resulted in many deaths. Many deaths!"

"We did as we were bidden."

Maura strode down the steps of the dais. "Did even one of you counsel Lady Jezra to open the city and welcome me as her royal sister?"

Another noble popped his head up. "We were forbidden to see Lady Jezra. The Hasan Daegian Mikkotto refused our every effort to see her."

"So, you admit to failure?"

"We failed, Empress Maura!" they cried.

"Should you be punished for this treachery and failure?"

They stared at the floor, not answering.

Maura turned and went back to her throne. "I am

fatigued by war. I wish no more of death." She waved the royal fan wearily. "But there must be punishment for wrongdoing. An example must be set, and a price will be paid. You, the nobles of Bhuttan, acted without prudence, and without any evidence of the charges leveled against me.

"Let this be law. I, Maura de Magela, tenth queen of Hasan Daeg, Empress of the Bhuttanian Empire, Great Mother of Kaseri, declare those kowtowing before me now to be enemies of the state. You are to serve as lowly field workers on the most northern estates of Bhuttan. Your wives, concubines, livestock, property, and wealth shall be transferred to other great houses — the ones who remained loyal to the House of de Magela. Your children shall be hung by the neck until dead in a public place so there will be no revenge wars in the future. Your houses will cease to exist. All this shall be carried out until the pleasure of the Empress is withdrawn."

A great gong sounded, drowning out the wailing of the disloyal courtiers.

Gitar, Iegani, and Chaun Maaun remained expressionless.

Maura snapped her fan shut.

The weeping nobles were led out by Hasan Daegian warriors.

Maura stepped off the dais and faced Gitar, Iegani, and Chaun Maaun. "My Empress, Lord Prince, and Duke Iegani. I bow to you three times to demonstrate the respect and gratitude we owe to you and the Dinii. May our paths always intertwine with peace and fellowship."

Maura bowed, as did the rest of the court.

"Bow," called out a herald. "All bow."

After the third bow, Maura returned to her throne.

Gitar stood and addressed the court. "Empress Maura, daughter of my heart. The Dinii and I have fought the brave fight alongside you. We have lost many comrades, but we shall begin anew. My advice to those remaining in court is to let go of the past and act for the future. What great things you can accomplish if acting for the common good. It is my greatest hope that *peace* will reign as *queen* in your hearts. As for those Bhuttanians who still feel the need to fight—direct your anger towards injustice, hunger, and poverty.

"I and my kind will fly to the Forbidden Zone. There we will rebuild our civilization. It is our hope that when next we meet, friendship will extend on all sides.

"Empress Maura and I have signed a new treaty between our peoples to express our devotion to peace. May your gods and goddesses protect and guide you thus. We leave Kaseri in good hands."

Empress Maura stood as well and bowed once more.

As Gitar was helped down from the dais, she paused by Maura, who was still bowing. "My sweet little sparrow. May your goddess Mekonia be a comfort to you."

"Goodbye, second mother of my heart."

Gitar stepped off the dais. Helped by Chaun Maaun, she passed through the congregation, who made a path for her as they bowed in respect as well.

Iegani stopped in front of Maura. "*Little sparrow?*" he said telepathically. "*Should be little dragon, no?*"

Maura fought the urge to smile.

Yeti, Toppo, and Benzar followed Iegani.

Out of the corner of her eye, Maura saw them leave little tokens for her at the foot of her throne. As they passed by, their wings brushed Maura's arms. That was their way of saying goodbye.

Maura and the entire court remained bowing until the Dinii left the palace and they heard Empress Gitar call to her warriors. One by one, they joined her in the sky and silently flew away to the Forbidden Zone.

42

Alexanee ventured to the dungeon.

Snarling, he demanded that the door to Mikkotto's cell be opened.

"I have orders that no one is to see her," claimed the guard.

"Surely you realize that doesn't apply to me."

"It doesn't?"

"Ah, hand over the key, you impudent fool."

The guard reluctantly handed the key to Alexanee.

"Now go away, and speak of this to no one."

The guard agreed, not wishing to get into trouble.

Alexanee opened the door and strode into the gloomy cell with his hand on the hilt of his sword. "Couldn't they at least give you a candle?"

Mikkotto emerged from a dark corner. Her clothes were in tatters and bits of straw matted her hair. "They do, but the guards steal them." She shrugged. "Have you come to separate my head from my shoulders? I should have known Maura would prefer such an atrocity to be committed in the dead of night."

Alexanee harrumphed. "As if murdering a wounded queen lying in the arms of her husband was not an atrocity."

"Maura exaggerated my culpability regarding the unfortunate death of her mother. After all, Dorak was there. He should have controlled his men better. I was merely a bystander."

Alexanee laughed. "You are a wonder. Even at the bitter end, you lie through your teeth with such audacity, it is as if you are gathering flowers in a field."

"If you are not here to kill me, why have you come?"

"Don't flatter yourself that my intentions might be of a carnal nature. I have read reports on your pursuits of pleasure. They don't appeal to me at all."

"Then what?" asked Mikkotto, her interest piqued.

Alexanee threw a dagger onto the straw floor. "There is a secret way out. After you kill the guard, take his keys and travel the hallway to the left. You will come to a metal door. It looks like it hasn't opened in a hundred years. Use one of the keys to open the door. Traverse the tunnel. It empties out into an abandoned field. A horse and a satchel of supplies will be waiting for you."

Mikkotto merely glanced at the knife. She was familiar with this old trick. She was supposed to go for the knife, and then Alexanee would kill her, citing self-defense.

"How am I to kill a guard using that tiny dagger?"

"I'm sure you will find a way."

"Why are you helping me to escape?"

"I want Maura preoccupied with searching for you. I have plans of my own, and do not want her poking around in my affairs."

"And what might those be?"

"My plans are of no concern to you. Use the dagger or not. Escape or not. I will waste no more of my time with you." Alexanee turned and left the cell. "Guard, I'm finished with this prisoner. Lock the door."

Alexanee watched as the guard locked the cell door. "Make sure you keep an eye on her. It's true what they say. She's a devil."

"A what, my lord?"

Alexanee shook his head sadly. "Obviously, you've never been to Anqara."

"No one has for many years now, my lord. People say it's haunted."

The general thought back to the razing of Anqara. It

had been a miscalculation on Zoar's part, for sure. If Zoar had established a more benign policy, Dorak and not Maura would be ruling in the Imperial Palace.

He had to respect Maura. Still so young, and yet she had outfought and outwitted them all. She deserved to be empress.

At least for the time being.

43

A trumpet sounded.

Bells, flutes, and drums accompanied a caravan of Sivan merchants guiding borax laden with expensive goods and richly-decorated wagons exhibiting many colorful flags. Behind the wagons rode many warriors on Hasan Daegian ponies. They were almost naked, wearing only thin tunics that came to their mid-thighs, metal helmets, and sturdy leather boots with steel toes. Each woman carried a sword, a bow slung over the saddle horn and several daggers secreted in their boots.

The people of the steppes didn't know what to make of this procession. Was this a military expedition coming to rampage through their community? Was this a simple trading caravan, and the women employed by the Sivans?

An elderly woman, moving stiffly due to arthritis,

emerged from a mustard-colored yurt. Men gathered around her as she forged ahead to greet the caravan. Recognizing the Bhuttanian royal crest on one of the wagons, the woman bowed, as did the men.

The wagons stopped, and a blue-skinned noble emerged from one, casually fanning herself. She wore simple white robes, and black hair fell unrestrained down her back. On her feet were leather slippers sheathed in gold leaf.

The elderly woman ran over to Maura and kowtowed, pleading, "Do not kill my son. Please spare him, Great Mother."

Maura, not understanding the woman's language, asked, "Does anyone know what she's saying?"

"I do," said a voice, thick with dangerous undertones. The spylord pushed his way through the nomads.

"Lord KiKu, I see you have put on some weight."

"She's pleading for you not to kill her son."

"So, Timon is still clinging to life. I worried that I might not arrive in time. Please tell Prince Bes Amon Ptah's mother that I have come to heal her son—not to kill him."

KiKu pulled the old woman up from her knees and translated Maura's response to her.

"Ah," she said, her head bobbing like berries dancing in boiling in water.

"She doesn't seem overjoyed."

"I told her that you came to pay your respects before Timon dies."

"Why would you tell such a lie?"

"It's better than getting her hopes up in case your efforts fizzle."

"You are too familiar with me, spylord, but I will give you something to be joyful about." Maura beckoned with her fan.

KiKu's eyes brightened as a door to another wagon popped open, and KiKu's four wives tumbled out.

Tippa and Tippu ran to KiKu crying out his name. "Lord KiKu. Lord KiKu!"

Madric and Pearl followed at a discreet distance, smiling broadly. Reaching KiKu, they waited until he acknowledged them. Bowing very low, they declared, "Lord KiKu, blessings upon you. Salutations from your wives."

With Tippa and Tippu still clinging to him, KiKu leaned forward and kissed both the older women on the cheek. "Blessings to you as well, my honored wives."

"Prince KiKu, we have a surprise for you," Pearl informed.

"Ah?"

Pearl turned and pointed.

Following her gaze, KiKu saw a young, beautiful

woman walking toward him, holding Akela's hand. He squinted, and then rubbed his eyes. "Can it be she escaped when Dorak murdered his father's concubines? KiKusan?"

The woman dropped the little boy's hand and rushed to KiKu. "It is I, KiKusan, Father."

"But how? Dorak had all Zoar's concubines and their offspring killed."

"I pretended to drink the poison and acted as if I was dead. When the guards were not looking, I rolled under a pile of blankets and made my escape when night fell. The guards lost count of how many women Zoar had, thus they did not come looking for me."

"But how did the empress find you?"

"Madric spied her," declared Tippu. "KiKusan was wandering in the bazaar, begging for food. She came up to Madric, and first wife recognized her."

KiKu grimaced. "You will never have to beg again, my daughter."

"That's because we're rich," Tippa announced.

"We are?" KiKu asked.

Pearl explained, "Yes, husband. You have been granted Mikkotto Sumsumitoyo's estates, with all her servants and assets." She pointed to the caravan's borax munching on grass. "Many of those wagons are loaded with silk cloth, gems, and precious metal for us. The empress says her debt to us is paid."

"I have wronged my queen and insulted her good intentions. I must apologize for my wrongdoing." KiKu turned around in all directions but could not find Maura.

Where was the empress?

44

Maura unclasped the amulet.

Carefully tucking the jeweled pendant in the sleeve of her robe, she said, "You won't be needing the amulet any longer, my good prince." She leaned closer. "Timon, can you hear me? It is your queen, Maura."

"Forgive me if I don't bow," croaked Timon, his voice barely audible.

Maura returned a whisper of a smile. "All is forgiven."

Timon struggled for breath as he spoke. "It is good of you to come to say goodbye, but there was no need. I am a contented ghost. I helped cast the Bhuttanian yoke from the necks of my people. I die a man who has done right in the sight of the nameless god. I have only one regret."

"What is that, royal scribe?"

"I wanted to go back to Bhuttani and find a veiled girl with bright green eyes. I never asked her real name. I'd like to know and maybe kiss her again. Maybe kiss her more than once. She had such lovely eyes."

"Hush, royal scribe," cooed Maura as she clasped Timon's hand tightly. "Hush, while I give you the gift of the Mother Bogazkoy."

45

Dorak had been sighted.

That's what was rumored from time to time. A Sivan saw him riding a magnificent steed on the road to Kaysia. A former Hasan Daegian diplomat swore she saw Dorak trudging on foot to Camaroon. A vagabond stated plainly he had shared stew with Aga Dorak at a campsite north of Bhuttani on the caravan route.

Maura had all sightings investigated and read the reports concerning Dorak carefully. But like dust blowing over a well-traveled road, the reports stirred the imagination, but in the end, there was no substance to any of the tales.

And so Maura would sit on her throne of bones . . . and wonder.

Also by
ABIGAIL KEAM

Princess Maura Tales

Josiah Reynolds Mysteries

Last Chance For Love Series

About The Author

Hello, my friend. I hope you enjoyed all five books of the Princess Maura Tales. I had such fun writing about Princess Maura and her adventures. If you like to read other genres, I also write *The Josiah Reynolds Mystery Series* and *The Last Chance For Love Series*, a happily-ever-after sweet romance series. I would love to hear from you. abigailkeam@windstream.net

If you like my stories, please leave a review and tell your friends about me.

Visit me at **www.abigailkeam.com**